A WEIRD PEACE

A WEIRD
PEACE
T. STYLES

ARE YOU ON OUR EMAIL LIST?

SIGN UP ON OUR WEBSITE

www.thecartelpublications.com

CHECK OUT OTHER TITLES BY THE CARTEL PUBLICATIONS

SHYT LIST 1: BE CAREFUL WHO YOU CROSS
SHYT LIST 2: LOOSE CANNON
SHYT LIST 3: AND A CHILD SHALL LEAVE THEM
SHYT LIST 4: CHILDREN OF THE WRONGED
SHYT LIST 5: SMOKIN' CRAZIES THE FINALE'
PITBULLS IN A SKIRT 1
PITBULLS IN A SKIRT 2
PITBULLS IN A SKIRT 3: THE RISE OF LIL C
PITBULLS IN A SKIRT 4: KILLER KLAN
PITBULLS IN A SKIRT 5: THE FALL FROM GRACE
POISON 1
POISON 2
VICTORIA'S SECRET
HELL RAZOR HONEYS 1
HELL RAZOR HONEYS 2
BLACK AND UGLY
BLACK AND UGLY AS EVER
MISS WAYNE & THE QUEENS OF DC (LGBTQ+)
BLACK AND THE UGLIEST
A HUSTLER'S SON
A HUSTLER'S SON 2
THE FACE THAT LAUNCHED A THOUSAND BULLETS
YEAR OF THE CRACKMOM
THE UNUSUAL SUSPECTS
LA FAMILIA DIVIDED
RAUNCHY
RAUNCHY 2: MAD'S LOVE
RAUNCHY 3: JAYDEN'S PASSION
MAD MAXXX: CHILDREN OF THE CATACOMBS (EXTRA RAUNCHY)
KALI: RAUNCHY RELIVED: THE MILLER FAMILY
REVERSED
QUITA'S DAYSCARE CENTER
QUITA'S DAYSCARE CENTER 2
DEAD HEADS
DRUNK & HOT GIRLS
PRETTY KINGS
PRETTY KINGS 2: SCARLETT'S FEVER
PRETTY KINGS 3: DENIM'S BLUES
PRETTY KINGS 4: RACE'S RAGE
HERSBAND MATERIAL (LGBTQ+)
UPSCALE KITTENS
WAKE & BAKE BOYS
YOUNG & DUMB
YOUNG & DUMB: VYCE'S GETBACK
TRANNY 911 (LGBTQ+)
TRANNY 911: DIXIE'S RISE (LGBTQ+)
FIRST COMES LOVE, THEN COMES MURDER
LUXURY TAX
THE LYING KING
CRAZY KIND OF LOVE
SILENCE OF THE NINE
SILENCE OF THE NINE II: LET THERE BE BLOOD
SILENCE OF THE NINE III
PRISON THRONE

By T. STYLES

Goon
Hoetic Justice
And They Call Me God
The Ungrateful Bastards
Lipstick Dom (LGBTQ+)
A School of Dolls (LGBTQ+)
Skeezers
Skeezers 2
You Kissed Me Now I Own You
Nefarious
Redbone 3: The Rise Of The Fold
The Fold
Clown Niggas
The One You Shouldn't Trust
Cold As Ice
The Whore The Wind Blew My Way
She Brings The Worst Kind
The House That Crack Built
The House That Crack Built 2: Russo & Amina
The House That Crack Built 3: Reggie & Tamika
The House That Crack Built 4: Reggie & Amina
Level Up (LGBTQ+)
Villains: It's Savage Season
Gay For My Bae (LGBTQ+)
WAR
WAR 2
WAR 3
WAR 4
WAR 5
WAR 6
WAR 7
Madjesty vs. Jayden: Short Story
You Left Me No Choice
Truce: A War Saga (War 8)
Truce 2: The War Of The Lou's (War 9)
An Ace And Walid Very, Very Bad Christmas (War 10)
Truce 3: Sins of The Fathers (War 11)
Truce 4: The Finale (War 12)
Ask The Streets For Mercy
Treason
Treason 2
Hersband Material 2 (LGBTQ+)
The Gods Of Everything Else (War 13)
The Gods Of Everything Else 2 (War 14)
Treason 3
An Ugly Girl's Diary
The Gods Of Everything Else 3 (War 15)
An Ugly Girl's Diary 2
King Dom (LGBTQ+)
The Gods Of Everything Else 4 (WAR 16)
Raunchy: The Monsters Who Raised Harmony
An Ugly Girl's Diary 3
From Men To Monsters (WAR 17)
Pretty Kings 5
From Men To Monsters 2 (WAR 18)
A Weird Peace

WWW.THECARTELPUBLICATIONS.COM

A WEIRD PEACE

BY

T. STYLES

PUBLISHER'S NOTE:
This book is a work of fiction. Names, characters, businesses, Organizations, places, events and incidents are the product of the Author's imagination or are used fictionally. Any resemblance of Actual persons, living or dead, events, or locales are entirely coincidental.

Library of Congress Control Number:

ISBN 10: 1948373982

ISBN 13: 9781948373982

Cover Design: Book Slut Girl

First Edition

Printed in the United States of America

What up Fam,

Happy holidays! I hope and pray that this holiday season brings you all the love and joy your hearts can handle. As we get ready to enter into a new year, I wish for you an even better season than the last!

Aight, I'm not about to hold y'all in this letter since it is the Holiday season, and we got things to do! Man oh man...The foolery that T. Styles has cooked up for y'all in this one is next level! I absolutely love delving into the new characters that her twisted mind comes up with and in this novel, she does not disappoint! This story is fire!!! So, let the kids play with their new stuff and go on ahead and slide off to your best hiding spot to get into, *A Weird Peace*!

Now, let's shift our focus and keep in line with tradition. In this novel, we want to give love to,

Kendrick Lamar

If you are not currently familiar or even aware of who this is, please allow me to introduce him to you…Kendrick Lamar is a rapper/songwriter and actor. He is being held as one of the greatest rappers of all time. In 2018, Kendrick was awarded a Pulitzer Prize for music and is the only musician, outside of jazz and classical genres to receive this honor. Although Kendrick has been putting in work for years and has dropped six albums during his career, this year, Kendrick really took off and has quickly become a household name. I know we at The Cartel Publications absolutely love him and his music not just because it's rap, but because of what he stands for as well. We are 1000% looking forward to seeing him perform at the Halftime Show in the 2025 Superbowl! If you like rap/hip-hop, check out Kendrick's music!

Aight Fam, don't waste any more time messing with me, jump into these new characters and enjoy!

As always, love & light!

C. Wash
Vice President

The Cartel Publications
www.thecartelpublications.com
www.facebook.com/authortstyles
www.facebook.com/Publishercwash
Instagram: Publishercwash
Instagram: Authortstyles
www.facebook.com/cartelpublications
www.theelitewritersacademy.com
Follow us on IG: Cartelpublications
Follow our Movies on IG: Cartelurbancinema

#CartelPublications

#UrbanFiction

#PrayForCece

#KendrickLamar

#AWEIRDPEACE

Not everything is deep. Sometimes a nigga's
just jealous.
Peep the signs.
Heed the warning.
And run.

PROLOGUE

BALTIMORE 2013

It was Christmas time...

And so the cold air was kicking thirteen-year-old Lockland's ass as he ran down the street, size thirteen's pounding the pavement. His chest was on fire as he gripped the rolled-up bills and the small bag of drugs in his sweaty hands so tightly his knuckles ached. Behind him, thirteen-year-old Jalen's sneakers slapped at the concrete as his big body caught wheels, throwing him in what felt like an uncontrollable cruise mode.

"Lock, man—" Jalen huffed. Heavier and shorter than Lockland, his round face was glistening with sweat. "They comin', I hear 'em!"

Lockland didn't answer.

He just ran harder.

Faster.

On the surface it looked like they were running from nothing. Besides, the streets were quiet except for the sound of traffic and a few beeping horns in the distance. But then the world appeared to change...the sounds of many men shouting, screaming, and yelling grew close.

Too close.

The group consisting of fifteen of the worst Baltimore had to offer, all under the age of sixteen, bent the corner at the far end of the street, their voices carrying over the empty block.

"There they go!" One of them yelled.

Lockland's stomach dropped. *Keep running. Don't stop.*

But Jalen groaned, his voice shaky. "Man, I can't. I—"

"Shut up and move!" Lockland yelled, pushing through the pain in his side.

Somehow, some way, they were able to lose them again and that's when Lockland spotted it.

A black van parked against the curb up ahead. The windows were dark, the back doors hanging open just enough to invite their bodies. It was the kind of van people noticed but ignored...always there.

Always empty.

And for now available.

Lockland pointed at it, barely able to get the words out through his gasps.

"Let's get in there."

"I don't think we—."

"Trust me, Jalen."

Jalen didn't question him further as they shot across the street, Lockland grabbing the door and pulling it open wide enough for them to dive inside. The metal floor was cold, and it reeked of gasoline, stale smoke, and something sour.

The van rocked slightly under their weight, but they didn't care. Lockland dragged the door almost shut, leaving only a sliver of light to peek through.

"Shh," he whispered, his voice serious. They pressed themselves flat against the floor, their hearts pounding so loud they could hear it in their ears.

Outside, the shouting boys slowed as they ran past them, not a one aware that they were within their midst.

"Where'd they go?!"

"How the fuck do I know? Check the alley!"

Lockland held his breath, each second stretching longer than it should've. His side ached where his ribs pinched together, and sweat dripped into his eyes, stinging. Jalen wheezed softly, his chubby hands pressed against his stomach like he was trying to hold himself together.

A few minutes passed.

Silence.

"Think they gone?" Jalen whispered, his voice shaky.

"Bro, you gotta chill. Just...just wait."

Jalen wished he was as easy as Lock...wished he was as cool. But nothing ever seemed to work out for him and it had him concerned for his weight. Concerned about how people looked at him.

His brother was not only stronger than him, but also a constant reminder that he was not enough.

Jalen may have held one impression, but Lockland was on another plane altogether. He was in absolute fear of what was coming next.

Lockland's arms trembled as he adjusted himself, his shirt damp against his skin. Normally he didn't like wearing a shirt, even in the cold. Luckily he wasn't so careless today. It was freezing in the van, but the sweat made it feel even worse, like his body couldn't decide whether to shiver.

Overheat.

Or die.

If only he hadn't been pressed to get some money to buy his mother a gift, they wouldn't be in this predicament. In other words, robbing them young niggas was all his idea.

So naturally he would assume all blame.

Suddenly, the sound of a single pair of heavy footsteps startled both of them. The driver. A menacing figure rounded the front of the van, whistling softly to himself. It sounded eerie, dark, alarming. The door on the driver's side opened, and a moment later, the van roared to life.

Lockland's eyes shot to Jalen.

"Run," he whispered, already pushing the door open as quietly as he could.

His brother, not as fast, fumbled behind him and lost his footing. "Wait—"

But Lockland didn't hear him or wait, he was already out, landing on his hands and knees, dirt and gravel scraping into his palms. He scrambled up, his legs aching as he took off running, leaving the van far behind.

When he turned around, he noticed Jalen wasn't there, and the van was halfway down the block.

"What...wait! Jalen!" Lockland shouted, chasing after the van. His sneakers smacked against the pavement, but the van was faster.

"Stop!" Lockland yelled, his throat burning as he sprinted. "You gotta...you gotta stop!"

But it didn't.

The van roared down the block, the taillights fading as it turned a corner and disappeared into the night. Lockland slowed to a stop, his chest heaving, his legs numb. He bent over, his hands on his knees, gasping for air that wouldn't come.

In fact, he would be waiting many days to breathe.

Snow floated down soft and steady, dusting the street with white, though the slush near the curb was already filthy.

Once inside the three-bedroom apartment, it smelled of cinnamon and grease, the kind of stank that clung to clothes and walls for days if a window wasn't opened. In the gloomy living room, the only light came from the Christmas tree in the corner. The blinking red, green, and blue bulbs made everything feel off…too cheery for the news coming.

Forty-two-year-old, Cakes Carvell sat in her recliner, her 8-year-old daughter Memory between her knees on a pillow, hair grease open on the armrest. For the moment, she worked Memory's thick curls into neat braids, her hands slow and steady, the metal comb clicking gently as she parted the hair, forming neat rows.

Favoring Lisa Nicole Carson in her day, she was what they called voluptuous as she was all titty, all ass and all thigh, all of the time. She oozed sex so much that she could count on one hand the female friends in her life. And one of them she gave birth to...her daughter.

Women just couldn't take the pussy power Cakes seemed to throw folks way, so they kept their men at a distance.

Beside the recliner, her old sewing stand stood against the wall, its wooden legs sturdy but scratched, the fabric draped across it half-finished, a red dress she was making for Memory to wear at church on Christmas.

Every time a section of hair was collected, Memory would wince as if she were stabbed. But Cakes kept moving. There was too much to do to give the child repeated attention.

Suddenly the front door opened and slammed causing both Cakes and Memory to jump. Like he was on fire, Lockland stumbled inside, his brown face reddened from the cold, snow melting in his hair and on his thin jacket.

But what Cakes noticed first was that he was shaking.

Fear snatched the woman's soul. Shoving Memory aside she said, "Where's Jalen, son?"

Lockland blinked at her. "They...he...we was—."

"Where is he?"

"They took him. The van—" Lockland didn't know who took him to tell the truth. So he merged worlds. The young dope dealers he robbed and whomever drove the van. Yeah, they were in cahoots as far as he was concerned.

Cakes' hand froze. She sat up straighter, her warm inner thigh brushing against the side of Memory's head, her eyes narrowing. And then she remembered, her son's vicious ways.

Jalen was a fuck up.

Selfish.

Dangerous.

Of course this was all a ruse for him to stay out of trouble.

The real T she desired to know, was what had he really done.

Suddenly she calmed down.

The amount of times he bullied Memory alone was enough to make her question how she brought something so evil into the world. Her only relief outside of Memory who minded her most of the time, was Lockland.

He was easy to love.

Real easy.

When she was tired, he helped her clean the house. When her feet ached from making clothes for locals and rich people who found her skills perfect, he rubbed them. When she needed help with an order, he assisted her with the garments, creating stitches so well folks could no longer tell her work from his. And when she didn't have the energy to cook, Lockland prepared the meals.

He always gave.

Jalen always took.

So she loved Lockland more.

She knew it was wrong, but in her eyes, anyone who said parents didn't have a favorite was lying. She'd bet her life that if a car had to fall on one child, and a mother had two, she'd always choose the one she cared about the most every time.

Don't get it twisted.

Jalen wasn't the only son who fucked up her idea of a perfect family. Her first born, twenty-five-year-old Turner, was once a hardworking man who helped her around the house and with the rent for their three-bedroom apartment. But when he broke his back on a construction site, and was prescribed oxcy's, he made every excuse to need them ever since. Everything hurt. All the time. He even blamed shit without pain receptors like his toenails, just to get a pill.

Eventually she gave him to the night, as she couldn't bear to see him during the day.

Now he made his way home whenever he needed something and at times she was too weak to say no. Besides, firstborns were often given more grace.

But Jalen?

Nah, she was starting to despise that nigga considering everything he saw her go through with Turner.

In her mind, he should know better.

But he didn't.

"Stop it," she said flatly. "I'm sick of you stepping up for your brother when he wouldn't do the same for you."

Lockland moved forward, his legs shaky. "I swear! They took him! I tried to stop them but—."

"Shut up! I don't wanna hear about it no more." She sighed. "Now go to your room."

Lockland stared at her as his world began to spin. The floor creaked with each step as he walked away. Should he call the cops? Something considered a hood sin.

Done with everything, Cakes turned on the movie *It's a Wonderful Life*, and the soundtrack playing softly in the background felt out of place.

It was ironic.

His life didn't feel wonderful now.

Lockland sat in the dark, knees pulled to his chest, his back against the cold wall of his room. The only light came from the hallway under the door. The snow had stopped falling, but the air was still crisp, slipping through the cracks in the windows.

His mother didn't believe him.

She didn't believe him.

Why didn't she believe him?

The words cut deeper than anything he'd ever felt. He could hear her humming softly to Memory in the other room, like nothing was wrong when in his world everything was on the line.

Lockland's fingers dug into his palms so hard they left marks because Jalen was out there somewhere.

Alone.

Scared.

And if truth could talk it would say it was his fucking fault.

After thinking about it for a while, suddenly he had an idea. Maybe it was them boys who caused the man in the van to take his brother. The same boys that had chased them earlier.

They *had* to be involved.

Right?

He grabbed his thin jacket off the floor and pushed open his window into the night. Two baby stories up, the wind hit him hard as he landed feet first in the snow.

His sneakers sank immediately, cold ice swallowing his socks whole.

Since he and Jalen robbed them earlier, he knew exactly where to go to confront them straight up. The old basketball court next to the run-down church, where the chain nets rattled even when there was no wind.

In pretty good shape for a young boy, after no time, Lockland spotted them before he got close and could smell the weed in the air. They weren't deep as before, but still deep enough to take his life if they were inspired.

There were five of them, standing in a loose circle, laughing and talking like the world was theirs when his world was being crushed. The biggest boy, tall and thick with a scar that ran through his eyebrow, leaned against the chain-link fence causing it to buckle. Of course he would be the one to notice Lockland first. "Hold up, is this nigga crazy?"

The laughter stopped.

Everyone looked in the direction of his gaze. Including Big Boys' thirteen-year-old sister Shannon. Who everybody at the school called Big Butt Shan-Na-Na.

Lockland kept walking until he was close enough to see their faces, the light from the streetlamp turning their breath to smoke.

Now his idea seemed stupid.

Ill prepared.

But he couldn't turn back. "Umm…uh…one of y'all seen my brother?"

They all looked at each other and laughed. The sound was loud, mean, and it hit him in the gut.

"Your brother?" Big Boy said, pushing off the fence. His boots crunched against the ice as he stepped forward. "You mean that fat ass little nigga who stole our stash and then got snatched in that van?"

It was all the proof Lockland needed.

Lockland's fists balled up at his sides. "You took him. I know you did."

The boys laughed again, louder this time. Why weren't they taking him seriously? Lockland's face burned hot even though the air was freezing, which was another reason he preferred not to wear a shirt. He reached into his jacket pocket and pulled out the crumpled bills...and the drugs that was rightfully theirs. "Here," he said, holding it out. "Take it back. I don't want it. I just want my brother."

One of the boys snatched it from his hand, flipping through the damp bills with a smirk. "So this nigga really trying to die tonight," another boy said, nudging his friend. "Came all the way back just to give us our own shit? Like you doin' niggas a favor?"

"Like I said, I just want my brother back."

The biggest one tilted his head like he couldn't believe what he was hearing. "Aight, let me tell you what I'ma do. If you whoop me right now, you can keep the money and—."

"I don't want the money," he said, "I want my—."

"Again, if you can beat me I'll find out where your brother at and you can keep the paper."

It was obvious. They were bored and wanted Lockland to be the show.

"What happens if I don't?"

He took off his jacket as the response and Lockland figured it meant death. It was settled, he had to fight.

Lockland's pulse pounded in his ears as they cheered, circling closer like wolves. And so, he pulled his hands out of his pockets. His fingers were stiff from the cold, but he curled them tight, ignoring the sting. "Let's do it."

Big Boy shook out his arms like he was warming up. "Your funeral."

Lockland didn't see the first punch.

It slammed into his gut so hard his knees buckled, the wind rushing out of his body in one sharp blast. With one blow he folded Lockland over, forcing him to slam into the snow on all fours, choking as bile crept up the back of his throat.

They laughed, but it sounded far away, like he was underwater. Probably due to the eardrum hit Big Boy gave.

"Get up," he said standing over him. "Shoulda never came back."

Lockland pushed himself up, his arms shaking, his vision blurry. His ribs felt like they might crack, and his breath came in shallow gasps.

He swung anyway.

Lockland's fist hit the Big Boy's shoulder, but it didn't do much. Another Big Boy special caught him in the jaw, and he stumbled back, tasting blood in his mouth. This was starting to look like more of a bad idea as Big Boy punished him unmercifully.

The thing was there was a saying, the bigger they are the harder they fall. Now Big Boy didn't drop, but he was out of breath trying to punish Lockland into submission. And Lockland knew it too.

The blows came less and were not as powerful.

"Come on!" Lockland shouted, his voice raw. "Come on!"

This went on for ten minutes until finally Big Boy's legs felt like jelly. He had to save face or else he would drop from sheer exertion alone. Ultimately giving Lockland the credit.

"I'm tired of kicking your ass. Go home."

Lockland wiped the blood from his mouth with the back of his hand. "I'm not leaving until I know where my brother is."

Big Boy removed a gun and suddenly Lockland remembered he snuck out and should go see about his mother.

Sure the fight yielded no information, but it didn't stop his hunt.

And make no mistake, he was hunting.

Night after night, as Jalen remained missing, Lockland's relentless pursuit left Cakes on edge. Her nerves frayed as she watched him come home with fresh scars, evidence of confrontations he refused to avoid. Even a few local mothers warned her that if Lockland didn't stop, he'd eventually get hit with something for which there was no cure.

"Lockland, I'm begging you," Cakes said coming into their room. "Please don't go out there looking for that boy. Trust me, he will be back. And you mean more to me than I can explain."

He knew she was speaking the truth, because she told him repeatedly how much she cared for him. But the guilt kept him hungry. So he kept looking and kept confronting anybody he figured had an answer.

Lockland lost the first fight.

He lost the next one too, and the one after that. But he kept returning, wanting to know where Jalen went.

It made it worse when Cakes finally called the police, and they deemed Jalen a runaway because he had gotten into so much trouble they assumed he had merged into the night. Despite being obligated to take a report anyway.

Days continued to flip by.

As the sun dropped and rose repeatedly, the bruises piled up on Lockland's face but so did the respect. His jacket got dirtier, his lip stayed split, and his hands wouldn't stop shaking.

But they stopped laughing at him.

They stopped asking why he cared so much. Instead, they just respected his focus. His loyalty.

Five days later, Lockland's name was on every corner, every block. And every hitter that mattered knew he was official. So they started leaving him alone and hired him for the underwork most didn't want to do instead.

Even his new girlfriend Shannon, Big Boy's sister, finally said yes to his requests for her number.

"Lockland," they'd whisper with respect when he walked by or in all the circles. A job here...a job there...and whatever innocence he'd had left, carried off in the snow.

FIFTEEN DAYS LATER

It was a cold day when Jalen returned.

Turner found him. And Cakes knew if her oldest son had anything to do with discovering his whereabouts, that Jalen was in the worst holes Baltimore had to offer.

The day Jalen returned home was uneventful actually.

Cakes was sewing a suit for Lockland to wear to church, and she didn't even bother to look his way when he dawned her door. Instead she paid her oldest son before he bounced, to get his high of choice, and proceeded to focus on the suit.

She only sent Turner because she was growing afraid for Lockland's life, and she was no longer willing to gamble that he would survive. For her efforts, the smell Jalen brought with him was enough to turn her stomach.

Upon hearing the news, Memory and Lockland rushed to the door, hoping to see a light in Jalen's eyes.

No light could be found.

Just darkness.

"Hungry?" Cakes asked Jalen.

He nodded.

"The roast is stewing, and the cornbread will be ready in ten. Go clean up. You smell like death."

He nodded and walked toward his room. Lockland was so happy to see him his body literally rumbled. "I...I made your bed and stuff."

Silence.

"You want me to make you a plate?" Lockland continued, his way of saying he was sorry. Sorry for leaving him in the van. And sorry for not finding him.

Jalen didn't respond. Instead he knocked past him and his kid sister on the way to his room.

He didn't say where he'd been.

And so folks stopped asking. His face was bruised, his lip split, and something was different about the boy's soul. He didn't speak much. When he did, it was short, sharp...like he was holding back worse things for the right time.

Lockland watched him closely.

Both for any indication that his brother wanted to be his friend again and also to be sure he wasn't in any danger. That night in the van had changed both of them, and though no one said it, Lockland knew things would never be the same.

It took a week, but Lockland finally managed to get through to Jalen.

It happened when he had almost given up trying.

Lockland and Shannon sat outside on the porch of the apartment building, the evening's cool air carrying the fragrant scent of fried food from someone's kitchen. He was sitting between her legs, as her fingers gently ran through his hair. He leaned back more and more. It was his way of feeling the warmth steaming off her quiet place, that he had been trying to dig into ever since they met.

"We gonna be together forever?" She asked.

"I 'on't know about all that right now."

She frowned. "Boy, what? You supposed to say yes."

"I don't wanna lie."

"Just play along."

He chuckled. "Okay, if I say yes then what kind of mother you gonna be?"

"The best mother anybody ever had," she smiled. "Trust me. I'll be just as good as your Cakes."

He nudged her and she hugged his neck as the building's door creaked open, and Jalen stepped outside, his shoulders slouched like the weight of the world was pressing down on him. Lately just his presence brought with it a bad mood.

For no real reason, he plopped next to Lockland without a word, his eyes darting to the ground.

"You hungry?" Lockland asked, holding up a paper bag. "I got you a pickle and some M&Ms."

Jalen glanced at it and nodded, snatching it from his grasp as if Lock would change his mind. He reached inside and pulled out the candy, unwrapping it quickly, like he would win a prize. One thing about Lockland, he always had junk food because Mr. Marcus at the corner store loved him.

Everyone loved him.

Why couldn't it be the same for J?

"You shouldn't be talking about getting pregnant," Jalen said out the blue.

Shannon frowned. "You were listening to my personal conversation?"

"I'm just saying...people think being a mother is sweet, when for real it ain't. You need a license for everything but mothering. How come?"

"J, we were just talking," Lockland said. "Lighten up."

He shrugged and downed half a bag of candy, his breath smelling like nuts. "I'm just saying she need to chill."

"And I'm saying you should leave her alone," Lockland said playfully.

When Jalen got quiet, Lockland gave Shannon the look, and she kissed him on the cheek and stood up. "Bye, Jalen."

"Bye."

She seemed to know what Lockland was about to do and gave him a soft smile before heading to her own house. Lockland watched her go before turning his attention back to Jalen. "You wanna play ball?"

Jalen shook his head without looking up, popping an M&M into his mouth. He felt he was too fat for all that athletic shit.

"You just wanna chill?"

Jalen finally looked at him, his voice quiet. "Is that okay?"

Lockland nodded, wishing Jalen would say more but grateful for progress. Because in is mind, the silence between them wasn't heavy, it felt like a start.

Suddenly Cakes pulled up with Carl behind the driver's seat blasting *Adorn by Miguel.* When she exited the car, he waved at the boys.

"How you doing, Jalen?"

Jalen rolled his eyes.

"What's up, Lock?"

"Hi Mr. Carl!"

Jalen high key glared at Lockland's kindness as the man pulled off. Wearing jeans and a white t-shirt, even in her forties Cakes had hips and body for days as she stepped closer, peach cream scented lotion rising from her skin.

The first thing she did was hug Lockland, her arms warm and firm as she pressed a kiss to his cheek. He always loved her embraces, more than he could say.

Jalen shook his head slowly.

"I saw your report card today, Lock," she said, her voice filled with pride. "Your grades are real good."

Jalen shifted in his seat, clutching the candy bag tighter. "Mine didn't come, ma."

Cakes' expression hardened, and she turned to him. She wasn't even talking to his uneducated ass. "I know it didn't. Because along with them fifteen days you were gone, you keep missing class. What's wrong with you?"

Jalen's face flushed, and he shot to his feet, running back into the house without another word. The screen door banged shut behind him, the sound hanging in the air.

Cakes sighed and sat next to Lockland, pulling him against her side with one arm. The warmth of her embrace eased some of the tension in his shoulders.

"I know you think I'm mean to him sometimes," she said, her voice softer now, "You probably right. But you gotta understand. When I had him, I was with a man who was dragging me down. We were both on drugs. Although I'm not anymore, the damage is still done. And some of that damage is Jalen." She sighed. "I just...I wanted it to be different for him. But I don't trust him. And you shouldn't either."

"Is that man, Mr. Carl?"

"My secrets are my secrets. Just know that it ain't been easy."

Lockland turned his head to look at her. "I understand."

"You a good one, Lockland. That's why I love on you so hard. But in a while..."

Silence.

"Are you okay, ma?"

She nodded. "Let's just say I just seen grandma and she not doing good. And I got a feeling after some time I won't be either." She breathed deeply. "So can you be strong for me, Lockland? Especially if something happens to me."

He nodded and she raised his chin. "I'll do anything for you. Never let no one disrespect you. Or hurt you."

"That's my favorite, baby," she said with a sad smile, kissing his cheek again before standing and switching into the house, causing the men across the street to grab their dicks as they took in the curves of her body.

They weren't the only ones watching. From the window, Jalen watched everything, his eyes dark with jealousy.

Jalen had gotten worse.

To put it frank the nigga was different.

The fights with strangers.

The fights with Lockland.

And taunting and teasing Memory so badly, that she would often yell out in pain whenever they were alone, causing Lockland to forbid her from being with him unless he was present. Which was hard because she truly loved him.

Jalen began to despise the bond Lockland continued to build with Cakes and he wanted him to know it too.

In the beginning Lockland did all he could to keep the peace, but it became obvious he didn't want it that way. He wanted war.

So they sparred.

When Jalen was out in the streets for those fifteen days, the house felt quiet, almost peaceful. But now that he was home, the two were at each other's throats every day, sometimes leaving bruises and blood behind. It made Cakes wonder if she could handle having them both under the same roof.

So when Jalen got into the tenth fight at school, which was more like a massacre considering he used a weapon, something had to change.

The small bedroom felt suffocating, its walls closing in with the weight of Cakes' anger still hanging in the air. Jalen sat slumped on the bed, his fists clenched tightly on his lap, with a soiled bloody tissue. The white t-shirt he wore was speckled with red dots, showcasing the secrets of earlier. The fresh bruise on his jaw and the swollen cracked lip felt more like a balloon against his body than anything else.

In his mind, if only he stabbed him with the knife he stole from home and kept moving, he wouldn't have seen him, and the kid would not have landed a blow nowhere near Jalen's face.

But the boy did get out on him because Jalen couldn't wreck unless he was bullying. So he used a pipe and ruined the kid's facial features instead.

While he thought about what he shoulda, woulda, coulda did, Lockland lingered by the door, holding a glass of red juice in his hands. Shirtless per usual, a pair of jeans hung on his hips. He had gotten more muscular while Jalen had gotten wider.

Watching Jalen, Lockland didn't say anything at first.

Just watched his brother in silence. The faint sound of crickets drifted in from the cracked window as he walked further inside.

"Here," Lockland finally said, stepping forward and extending the glass of strawberry Kool-Aid toward Jalen. "Figured you'd want this."

"How come you don't never got no shirt on?"

"You jealous?"

Silence.

"Why you bring this to me?" He mumbled, though he still snatched the glass. "You know I'm not supposed to drink nothin' but water."

"Because I wanted to. And you my brother."

Jalen shook his head and rolled his eyes. "Listen, she already think I'ma problem. Don't need you in here making shit worse."

Lockland sighed and leaned against the wall next to the slightly open window. "You got into another fight, J. First with me then with whoever that was at school. Like what the fuck is you doing? Are you trying to make her mad?"

"You called me kicking your ass a fight?"

"I let you get one in on me. You and me both know that ain't how it usually goes down."

"Lies. Even if it was true, why you do that?" He said slyly before walking over to him, on the opposite side of the window, the floorboards creaking under his weight.

"You know why. Because if I hit you, I'ma hurt you. And I don't wanna do that."

Silence held the room hostage.

"Listen, like I said, you gotta stop giving her reasons to beef with you."

Jalen shook his head and took a long swig before setting it on the windowsill. "I'm not gonna let nobody call me...call me—."

"Fat? Because if you wanna lose weight I can show you how I—."

"I don't want you teaching me shit, nigga!"

Silence.

"J, you can be mad at me all you want. I mean, I told you I tried to find you when you were gone, and you probably hurt by that shit. But I did try and—."

"So you got a new girlfriend, rolling with Wakes, Dion and Shoes because you wanted to find me? Yeah aight."

"Trust me...you don't wanna know the shit I did out there to find you. But I really do feel like you hit that boy in the face with a pipe to get at me because you jealous or something. They saying he might need facial surgery."

"Why would I be jealous of you, nigga? You want my life, remember?" He grinned. "Trust me...I see how you be around here. Kissing on mama, looking after Memory, all to make me the villain."

"That's not true."

Jalen pushed the window open wider, letting the night air flood the room. A car playing *Bitch Don't Kill My Vibe*, bumped in the distance but suddenly he heard something else.

"Hold up, you hear that?" Jalen whispered.

"Hear what?"

Jalen leaned against the windowsill, his head tilted slightly as if he was listening for something beyond the sounds of the night. Lockland joined him. Outside, they could hear Cakes' voice drifting up. She was speaking to a neighbor, standing directly under the window, her voice heavy with frustration.

"I'm so sorry about all this shit," Cakes said, her voice cracking. "Jalen been acting out lately and I don't know how to control him. But if you sue me—."

"My child gonna need surgery and that's all you can come up with?"

"I don't mean to be insensitive, Lala. But I don't know what to do anymore. And with Memory being impressionable I'm afraid...of having Jalen around." Her voice trailed off, but the concern was clear.

Jalen's shoulders stiffened at her words. "She's always apologizing for me. Like I'm some kind of burden."

Lockland shifted uncomfortably. "Maybe you could—"

"What...say sorry? Like that'll change anything. She thinks I'm the problem, so I'll be the problem."

"What does that mean?"

The sound of Cakes' voice rose again, sharper now. "I just...need some time. I have to think about Memory and Lockland. But I'll sell my car and give you what I can."

"Girl, you gonna have to do that. Because I'm not gonna have my boy all fucked up out here."

Jalen froze, his grip tightening on the glass. Lockland moved toward him, his hand reaching out. "J, she doesn't mean it like that."

The words barely left his mouth before Lockland accidently knocked the glass out of his hand. Time seemed to slow as the glass tumbled off the edge, and out of the window. Seconds later, a piercing cry sliced the air. Both boys leaned out the window, as Cakes stumbled back, clutching her cheek, blood streaming through her fingers from a long, jagged cut.

"Oh my God," Lockland breathed, backing away from the window. "It was an accident. I didn't mean to—"

It took a few moments, but the door burst open, and Cakes stormed in, covered in blood. "What happened?" She rushed in their direction, blood pouring between her fingers.

Lockland stepped forward, his hands raised in surrender. "It was an accident. We—."

"I can't do it no more with you two," she said holding her face. "I just can't."

"Ma, don't say that," Jalen begged. "It was an accident and—."

"Don't lie to me!" She snapped, her eyes darting to Jalen. "It was you, wasn't it? You mad at me because I punished you. And you threw a glass at me?!"

Jalen's mouth opened, but no words came out. Not only was it an accident, but it was Lockland's fault. "Ma, I would never hurt you like that. I—"

"We were talking by the window!" Lockland yelled. "And—"

"Enough!" She shouted, cutting him off before focusing on Jalen. "I'm done with you. The fights. The bullying your sister. It all ends today."

"We didn't mean to—."

"Be quiet, Lockland. He's got to get out of my house. Even if I didn't want to, the police gonna see to that after what happened today at school. Now do you prefer for me to put you out instead?"

Lockland felt the floor drop from up under him.

"Because I can't pay for no more surgeries. I can't pay no more fines because y'all two are holding onto whatever happened the day he went missing for fifteen days. It's either him or you so I want to know, who threw the glass at me?"

Lockland thought about his new girlfriend. He thought about his friends, and he thought about the money he was making on the streets.

"Tell her you did it, man," Jalen said with tears in his eyes. "Please, brother."

"I...I can't."

"It's settled," Cakes said as if relieved Lockland didn't come forward, "I'm calling child services before Lala calls them and the police—."

"Mama, please don't put me out," Jalen wept. "You don't...you don't know what I went through out there. I—."

"I'm sorry...but you made too many promises. Promises you couldn't keep. And in my eyes that means you ain't about shit."

"But I don't have anywhere to go."

"Not my problem. Not anymore."

Jalen took a deep breath. "No need in calling CPS, I'm gone."

"I'm still gonna call them. Don't want them thinking I threw you out without getting you some help."

"Fuck you, bitch! I'm leaving. Don't wanna be in no dusty ass group home."

"If you leave without them knowing where you are, and I get in trouble you're dead to me."

"Well I guess you gonna have a hard time finding a ghost." Before leaving he took one last look at Lockland, "This is your fault and everything that happens after it, Mr. Favorite." He looked at his mother. "Because she finally chose you over me."

Lockland stepped forward. "J, wait—"

Jalen hesitated for a moment, his gaze flicking between Lockland and his mother. Then, without another word, he turned and rushed into the night.

A YEAR LATER

Shannon's room smelled like cocoa butter and cheap vanilla perfume. *New Flame* by Chris Brown played from a crackling speaker in the corner and barely filled the silence. Lockland sat on the edge of the bed, his sneakers clean enough to reflect the dim light from the lamp beside him. His jeans were without a wrinkle, his white tee spotless, and his fresh-cut hair shined slightly.

Shannon sat cross-legged on the floor beneath him, holding a small pillow tight to her chest like it could stop what was coming. Her long black hair draped both sides of her honey brown face. Mostly perfection, she had a piece of thread hanging on her shirt which was sending him, but he didn't wanna feel like he was ignoring her by pulling it off.

He was a clean and neat freak these days.

Shannon's voice was soft, pleading. "You don't gotta do this, Lock."

He leaned forward and touched her cheek. His fingers were smooth and dry, the knuckles still faintly red from a fight two weeks back. "Listen, I gotta find my brother. And I don't want you to be scared for—"

"Lock-land...duh," she said, her words always sounding as if she were singing when she was whining. "For why though? You heard what Big Boy said. He's gone. Let it stay there."

"I feel like...I kinda feel like this is all on me."

Her shoulders slumped. "Is Cakes even asking for him?"

"Nah...but I know she feel guilty. I hear her crying sometimes at night."

He grabbed her hand, and she rose and sat face to face on his lap, her knees pressing against her mattress. The warmth of their bodies against each other. Seeing the thread, he pulled it off and cupped her ass. "You know the kind of nigga you got. I gotta find J. So let me do me and stay out the way."

"You wanna smoke before you leave?"

"So I can be bumping off the walls again? And so you gotta call Wakes and 'em to come get me. That sounds like fun to you?"

With that, he kissed her forehead softly and pat her ass for her to rise. When they were standing face to face, he kissed her lips. Next he sniff his finger and winked after thinking about the finger fucking they just did.

"Pussy always fresh."

"Shut up, boy," she blushed.

Before she could say anything else, he moved to the window, sliding it up carefully so it wouldn't creak. The cold air hit him like a slap, but he barely noticed as he slipped into the night.

The crack house stank like sweat, smoke, and stale piss. The walls were streaked with dirt, the kind that didn't wipe off, and the windows were covered with sheets that let no light or hope inside.

And yet Lockland stood in the doorway as of none of it mattered as he witnessed his older brother Turner who was sprawled on a thin mattress, shirtless and shivering under a worn blanket.

His face was gaunt, his eyes sunken deep into his skull while a pipe sat next to him, still warm.

"Turner," Lockland said, kicking him softly.

Turner opened one eye, squinting against the vague light from the hallway. "What you doin' here, man?" His voice cracked, rough and weak.

Lockland ignored the question. "Where's Jalen?"

Turner coughed, a sharp, ugly sound that rattled in his chest. He wiped his nose with the back of his hand, sitting up slowly. "Why you care? You don't need to see him. Leave him alone, Mr. mama's favorite. He ain't your problem."

Lockland's jaw tightened. "I need to find him. It's been a year and—"

"Man, let it go." Turner's voice dropped to almost a whisper, his eyes darting around. "He too far gone, just like the rest of us."

"You know what, I know what you wanna hear." Lockland pulled a wad of cash from his pocket and tossed it onto the mattress. The bills fluttered and stuck to Turner's damp skin. "Now, where is he?"

"So the streets really crowned you huh? Almost fifteen and you got more money than most niggas ever seent in their lives." Turner stared at the money for a long time before snatching it up with shaky fingers. "If this what you want, just remember you ain't hear it from me." He stood up and almost rocked sideways into the wall. "He's sleepin' over at that old construction site on Mayfield." He wiped the cream-colored crust out of his eyes. "Him and some other niggas you don't wanna be nowhere near."

Lockland nodded and turned to leave but Turner's voice stopped him at the door.

"It ain't gonna change nothin'," Turner said, the words soft, almost sad.

The wind cut through the empty construction site like a knife where a half-made house was propped.

The air smelled like wet concrete and old ash, the ground still dusted with snow that crunched under Lockland's sneakers. He moved between rusted machinery and broken cinder blocks until he spotted them in the half-finished bedroom.

Several figures curled up on flattened cardboard, half-hidden under torn blankets and old coats. Their breathing was slow, heavy, like the weight of the cold air was pressing on their lungs. He walked carefully, still not seeing who he came for. It took some time and then he spotted him.

Jalen sat slumped against a concrete wall, his thin body wrapped in a tattered coat two sizes too big. His face was hollow, the flesh dark and tight against his cheekbones. His lips were cracked and from his position, it looked like someone was sucking his dick under the heap of covers on his lap because they moved up and down as Jalen moaned.

"Jalen," Lockland whispered.

Jalen's eyes widened as he said, "Stop...stop..."

Suddenly the pile ceased moving as Jalen shoved it off.

Lockland stepped closer, his sneakers scraping the gravel. For a moment, they just stared at each other.

"Lock," Jalen said, his voice hoarse, like it hurt to speak. He pushed himself up slowly, wincing as he did. He had lost some weight, but didn't appear healthy. "Look at...look at you. Still clean though." He stood in front of him. "Always clean. Like life and my mama been treating you good."

Lockland shifted a little. "Who was that?"

"Nobody. What you talking about?" He grinned.

Lockland didn't smile.

His mood was off considering how they last saw each other. "I came to find you." He looked at the pile again trying to see who would reveal themselves.

"And do what with me?"

Lockland didn't have an answer. "Maybe put you up in a place for a while. I been making some money so I wanna look out."

"Put me up, huh. Like I'm your bitch?" Jalen smirked. "That guilt still eatin' you alive, huh? How you lied on me and had mama throw me out."

Lockland shifted a little.

"If it's forgiveness you want...you got it."

His spirit told him that the forgiveness came from a place unpure, but it was what he wanted to hear, and so he ignored the signs.

Jalen moved even closer, and the smell of his skin hit Lock. Smoke, sweat, and something sour underneath it all. The coat was stained, his hands dirty, but Lockland wrapped his arms around him anyway, pulling him into a dap followed by a hug.

"Why you living like this? A group home gotta be better than this. I—."

"How the fuck you sound? You don't know what it's like to live in a group home," Jalen snapped, his eyes moving wildly in his head. "So don't say that shit again."

Lockland's body tensed, his clean shirt brushing against Jalen's filthy coat. When they pulled apart, Jalen's smile was gone. His eyes narrowed slightly, his face turning into a frown.

"How's Memory?" Jalen asked suddenly, his voice soft but inquisitive.

"She's good. Why?"

Jalen nodded, his gaze lingering on Lockland a little too long. "I wanna see her too," he said, his voice almost a whisper. "Tell her I'm sorry about all the things I put her through."

Silence.

Nothing but the wind blowing between them. And a man, who was sitting near the pile of clothing that was once on his lap, looking in their direction.

Lockland's chest felt tight. Something didn't feel right, but he couldn't put his finger on it. "We'll see."

"Make it happen. You owe me that."

The hum of the old sewing machine filled the room, its rhythmic *clack-clack-clack* blending with the faint smell of thread, worn wood, and Cakes' peach hand cream lotion. Lockland sat across from her at the sewing table, carefully folding a dark piece of fabric. His hands were steady, his long fingers pressing creases just like she'd shown him.

"Groceries are in the fridge," he said quietly, glancing up.

Cakes scratched her bubbly cleavage and paused for a second. The light from the table lamp caught her big, beautiful eyes, and the raised scar on her face. "Don't know how you get money for—."

"Don't ask, ma."

She sighed deeply. "Than its best I say thank you," she said, her voice low but warm. "You didn't have to do it though."

Silence.

He just nodded and went back to folding the sleeve.

From the hallway, Memory's small voice broke the quiet. "Lockland, I'm ready!"

The girl stepped into the room, her hair done up in two neat braids with colorful beads clicking softly at the ends. She wore a puffy pink coat, too big for her small frame, but it made her look younger than her nine years.

"You got it from here, ma?" He stood up from the sewing machine.

"Go on. But when you get back we have to go grocery shopping."

He frowned and touched her shoulder gently. "Ma, I put groceries in the house already. Just told you that. Everything okay?"

She nodded. "Uh...I know that. Why you putting off like I'm crazy?"

Lockland looked her over for a moment and then focused on Memory. He kissed her cheek and almost didn't want to leave.

"I can stay if you want. We can watch some movies and—."

"No...go."

His heart broke seeing her like this.

"Alright, let's go. I'm takin' Memory to get somethin' to eat."

"But I took out the chicken for dinner and—."

"Won't be out long, I promise."

Cakes' smile faltered. "You sure that's all it is? You ain't lyin' to me?"

"Nah."

Cakes glanced up from her work, her hands slowing on the fabric. "Well you better get out there before the night catches you in a bad way."

He kissed her on the cheek again as Memory slipped her small fingers into his, and together they headed for the door.

AT THE RESTAURANT

The diner smelled like grease and old coffee, the kind of place where the windows always fogged up from the heat inside. The booth Lockland and Memory sat in was cracked along the edges, but the table was wiped clean. Lockland sat with Memory tucked close to his side, the steam from their food rising in front of them.

Across from them sat Jalen.

He looked different.

His clothes were clean. His face, though thinner, didn't look as hollow. His hands rested on the table, nails trimmed, though dirty as they fidgeted with the edge of a napkin.

"I miss you," Jalen said softly, his eyes moving to Memory.

Memory smiled, bright and wide. "I miss you too!" She grinned, before tucking her face into the side of Lockland's body in a bashful shy way. "You know what I've been doin' at school?"

Jalen nodded faintly, but his eyes darted toward Lockland, then back to Memory. "Nah...tell me."

She launched into a list of stories...how she'd read a whole book by herself, how her teacher gave her a gold star for answering questions, and how she'd drawn a picture of mama and Lockland for Christmas. As she spoke, her hands waved in the air, the beads at the ends of her braids clicking softly.

And that's when Lockland noticed.

Jalen wasn't listening to shit little shawty was saying.

He appeared not to have cared.

His eyes didn't focus on Memory. He sat still, too still, staring at something else, like he'd already left the conversation. What was he looking at?

Lockland.

Jalen's jaw twitched slightly, and his hand tore the edge of the napkin into thin strips. "Jalen," Lockland said, his voice low, a warning. "You good?"

"Yeah, why you say that?"

"Memory was talking to you but you looking at me."

Jalen's eyes flicked up, his face slipping back into a smile, though it didn't reach his eyes. "I'm listening, nigga," he said smoothly. "So what, the pretty boy can't take a little eye play?"

Eye play?

Lockland didn't respond. Instead he leaned back slightly, his arm still around Memory as she kept running her flaps nonstop. The only sunny side is that Memory didn't notice Jalen could care the fuck less, or else her feelings might be crushed. She was too excited, too happy to see her big brother again.

"Gotta hit the bathroom," Lockland said finally, sliding out the booth. "You gotta go too, Memory?"

"No, I wanna stay with Jalen for—."

"Come on and go to the bathroom," Lockland said trying to separate them for a moment. "I don't want you crying about it when we hit the road. We got a fifteen minute—."

"She wanna stay, man," Jalen said. "She *my* sister remember?"

Lockland shifted a little and said, "Okay." He had all intentions on pissing and coming out quick. Dick still wet if he had to because he didn't trust Jalen. "I'll be right back."

Jalen nodded, his smile lingering as Lockland walked off. The air in the bathroom was cold, the small window cracked just enough to let the winter in. He found and empty stall, closed the door quickly and walked into another due to shit being in the bowl.

When he was done pissing he washed his hands and dipped back into the restaurant.

What he saw caused him to freeze.

Jalen had slid over, sitting too close to Memory if you asked him. He didn't care if he was her brother. He was leaned over her, his hand resting on the table but his lips next to her ear. He looked predatory and Lockland's jaw tightened, his teeth grinding as he watched from a distance.

"Memory," he said, his voice stern as he approached.

She looked up, her smile still bright. "Hey, Lock! I was just tellin' Jalen about—"

"Fuck all that shit. Let's bounce," Lockland said, cutting her off.

Jalen leaned back, his smile lingering as Lockland grabbed Memory's coat. "She's fine. We were just talkin'."

Lockland ignored him. He helped Memory into her coat, his hand trembling slightly as he buttoned it up. "Say bye," Lockland told her.

Memory turned back to Jalen, her smile dimming just a little. "Bye, Jalen. I wish I could stay longer."

"You can't," Lockland said.

"Remember what I said right?" Jalen said to Memory.

"What you tell her?" Lockland asked, heated and angry.

"You still trying to take my place huh, Lockland?" Jalen interrupted.

"If it means protecting her, the answer is yes."

"Protecting her from what?" He grinned.

"You tell me."

Lockland grabbed Memory's hand and led her out, as the cold air hit them abruptly.

The restaurant door swung open with a groan, spilling the smell of grease and burnt coffee into the cold night air. Jalen stepped out, his hands shoved deep into the pockets of his sweater, his breath visible in the frigid air. He looked up and down the empty street, his dark eyes narrowing when he peeped two figures leaning against a broken-down car at the end of the block. When he spotted them with a head up nod, they moved in his direction.

It was Tink and Everett.

Two niggas who were up to no good, just like him.

Neither one of them had seen a comb or a toothbrush in a while as they all lived on the streets. Tink was flicking a lighter open and closed, the tiny flame dancing before disappearing again. His teeth clicked as he sucked on a toothpick as Everett stood with his back to the car, his breath fogging the air, shoulders hunched like the cold was settling into his bones.

Jalen's boots crunched on the snow-covered sidewalk as he approached. The closer he got, the more his smile returned, slow and smug.

"What's good?" Tink said, not looking up, his lighter sparking again.

Jalen stopped in front of them, the streetlight above showing them niggas in all their filthy glory. "I got somethin' lined up. That little plan we working on. We using Memory."

Everett frowned. "Hold up, you involving your little sis in this shit?"

"Why the fuck not?" He said, his voice low and smooth. "If she gonna help bring him out that's what we need right?"

Everett rolled his eyes, pushing off the car. "How you gonna get her to do that anyway?"

Jalen chuckled, shaking his head. "First of all she don't even know what she's doin'," he said, pulling his hands from his pockets and rubbing them together like the cold had just hit him. "I told her we'd hang out. She thinks she gonna wait for me outside."

Tink looked up from his lighter, his toothpick clicking between his teeth. "You serious?"

"On everything I'm serious. You know what's funny, for all that shit ma was talking about me, she still raised a dummy."

The way he said it...flat, like Memory was just another tool...hung heavy in the air for a moment. Everett shook his head and mumbled something under his breath, his boots scraping against the ice as he turned toward the car.

"That's your own sister, man," Everett said.

"You think I give a fuck?"

He turned and started walking, trekking through the snow as the other two fell into step behind him.

Memory had lied to her mother and Lockland because she missed Jalen.

And now that she saw how scary the neighborhood looked, she hoped she didn't make a mistake.

Her small sneakers crunched against the frozen ground as she walked up to the broken-down apartment building. The air smelled like old trash and something like flesh left to rot. She clutched the straps of her pink bookbag tightly, her hands cold even through her thin gloves.

The building stood tall, though battered, with cracked bricks and windows either covered by blankets or riddled with bullet holes. The front steps were chipped and crumbling, looking like they couldn't hold much more weight.

As she hesitated, the wind tugged at her coat as she stared at a rusted van parked out front. It looked familiar, though she didn't know why...dirty and dented, with its tires half-flat.

"Jalen," she screamed to the building, not sure where to go. "Jalen I'm here!"

After a few moments, the front door screeched open. Believing it was Jalen, she smiled until she saw a large man stepping outside. He was round in the middle, his big coat barely able to zip up.

He hummed as he moved, a soft, off-key tune that felt strange in a place so quiet. His boots scraped on the cement, each step slow, like he had nowhere to be except in the child's face.

Memory stood frozen, gripping the straps of her bag so tight her fingers ached.

The air shifted.

"You looking for somebody, little girl?"

She nodded yes.

"Your hands cold?"

She nodded yes again.

Softly he took them and pulled them toward him. Before long her hands were warm, but she felt something squishy between his legs. When she looked up at him, his tongue hung out the side of his mouth as he moaned.

What was she holding?

From the shadows at the side of the building, three figures stood. "I don't like how he looks," Everett whispered. "We going over there right now? Cuz what the fuck is he even doing?"

"Nigga, shut your bitch ass up," Jalen responded.

As the man readjusted Memory's hands, Jalen stepped out first, followed by Tink and Everett. They moved like a group, slow and deliberate, their eyes locked on The Whistler. Jalen's face was dark, not just in the hollow look of it, but something deeper, something cold and empty.

The man stopped humming. He turned, fear spreading across his face. "You said I could have her," he said to Jalen confusing his friends. "So why are you here to see me? I thought you didn't want—"

What did he mean *have her*?

"I ain't come to see you!" He said. "I don't even fuck with you!"

"What do you mean?" The Whistler continued. "I gave you some money all of two months ago and—."

Tink and Everett looked at one another. They were confused on the plan. As far as they knew they were coming to rob a man but now it appeared so much more was happening.

Even Memory was scared and covered her face with her gloves until she realized they stank.

"You took me! From my house for fifteen days! And only released me because you said I was too fat."

"Jalen, you and I were good. We had a relationship and—."

Jalen couldn't hear anymore.

Something awful had occurred.

He snapped.

The sound hit Memory first...flesh smacking against flesh, hard and sharp, followed by the Whistler's pleas for mercy. Jalen drove his fists into the man over and over, his shoulders jerking with every punch. It didn't take Tink and Everett long to join the show. The man's cries turned into gurgles as he fell against the steps, his body slumping to the ground.

As they continued to beat him into the concrete, their heavy breath filled the space between the blows and stomps. Seeing the violence, Memory's legs shook, her bladder released, and her knees knocked as she watched.

Jalen didn't stop.

He didn't care.

And this would have future issues with time.

As she bore witness, his face twisted with something she didn't recognize...something that scared her more than the blood spilling over the whistler's coat, dripping onto the ground in thick, dark drops.

"Stop," she whispered, her voice small, barely there.

But Jalen didn't hear her.

He didn't want to hear her.

The man groaned, trying to move, but Jalen grabbed his collar, slamming his head back down onto the step with a sickening *thud.* When his eyes rolled up into his head, Memory flinched, her chest tight, her stomach twisting like she might throw up.

Suddenly she backed up into the van that sat there, parked like it was watching, and then Memory remembered...Jalen had been taken.

This van.

Probably this place.

Something terrible had happened here.

She wasn't there but Lockland had mentioned the description many times when he was missing to their mother. That's why it was so familiar to her. It was during the times when she should be asleep, but she remained up wanting to know something...anything about her brother.

Who now resembled a monster.

When Jalen finally stopped, he stayed crouched over the man, his shoulders rising and falling, his bloody hands hanging limp at his sides. The man didn't move anymore. Silence settled over everything except Memory's breathing.

Jalen turned toward her, and for the first time, she saw his face clearly.

His eyes were empty.

He wiped his hands on his jeans, smearing the blood like paint. Then, slowly, he walked toward her. Memory stumbled back a step, her whole body shaking.

"Don't tell nobody," Jalen said, his voice low and rough. "There will be nightmares...still...say nothing." His bloody hand reached out, grabbing her coat sleeve, the red smearing against the hot pink fabric. "Do you hear me?"

Memory stared up at him, her mouth trembling.

She couldn't speak, couldn't move.

"*Don't tell nobody,*" he said again, his grip tightening just enough to let her know he meant it.

Her brother's bloody handprint on her coat, a stain she wondered if would ever wash out.

Memory yanked her arm free and turned, her sneakers slipping on the frozen ground. She ran, the wind cutting at her face, her pee now cold giving her chill as her bookbag bounced against her back. Tears blurred her vision, but she didn't stop.

Behind her, the apartment building seemed to grow smaller and darker, fading into nothing as she ran. Although she could still hear Jalen.

Laughing.

The smell hit Lockland before anything else.

Death's perfume...it was unmistakable.

It was the same odor Jalen returned home in when he was missing last year.

The kind of stench that clung to your clothes and skin, refusing to let go. Still, he crouched low, the air damp and heavy around him as he moved through the old storm drain. His boots splashed lightly in the shallow, murky water, the faint sound echoing off the concrete walls.

The place wasn't much.

A shit hole to be honest.

Just a forgotten part of the city's sewage system, barely big enough for someone to squat in without feeling trapped. But for Jalen, it was a perfect hiding spot. It was dark, cold, and filthy. A place only a desperate, on the run ass nigga would call home.

This is why he was there looking for Jalen.

After all, after exposing Memory to a murder, Lockland put the word out on the street that he was looking for him. And so the man did what he knew how to do.

Hide.

The thing was over the year, Lockland had gotten deeper in the streets too, and knew the places the scared people like Jalen would roam.

And so Lockland kept moving, his breath steady despite the ache in his legs from crouching so long. He didn't need light. He didn't need sound.

He just *knew*.

And there he was.

Jalen sat hunched near the corner of the drain, a small flickering flame from a lighter barely illuminating his face. His clothes were stained, his hands filthy, and his eyes were evil even in the dim glow. He looked up, startled, the lighter snapping shut in his hand.

"How the hell—" Jalen started, his voice hoarse.

Lockland straightened, his dark eyes steady as he stepped closer, the shadows clinging to him like armor. "You used your own sister as bait, nigga? And you thought I wouldn't find you?"

For a second, Jalen didn't move, his gaze darting to the small opening behind him. "So, what now?" Without waiting on a response, Jalen took off.

Thinner than he was before, but still slower, by the time they climbed out of the drain, a crowd had gathered. The word had spread fast...Lockland had found Jalen.

With plans to make him pay for what he did to Memory.

All the worst and best Baltimore had to offer were gathered.

Even Tink and Everett stood near the edge of the parking lot where they emerged, their faces tight with unease. Beside them was a boy named Antonio, tall and boney, his arms crossed as he watched the scene unfold. A few others lingered nearby, all getting excited about whatever was going down.

On the other side, Lockland's crew waited silently. The Dust Boys...Wakes, Dion, and Shoes...stood shoulder to shoulder, their clothes clean but wrinkled, their faces blank. They weren't there to fight, just to make sure no one else stepped in. Lockland had made that clear before they even left because he only wanted them to watch his back.

"Stay out of it," he'd told them, his voice demanding. "That's all I want you to do."

Now, the two brothers stood in the middle of the lot, the cold air biting at their skin as Jalen rolled his shoulders and cracked his neck.

"You doing all that shit for nothing," Lockland laughed.

"You sure you wanna do this?" Jalen responded.

Lockland was done talking. He would show him better than he could tell him. He just raised his fists and planted his feet firmly in the cracked asphalt.

Jalen moved first, his fist swinging wide.

But Lockland ducked, the motion smooth, almost effortless. He came up fast, his own punch connecting with Jalen's ribs. The sound was dull but sharp enough to make Jalen grunt, stumbling back a step.

This wasn't the little nigga from a year ago who fought on the basketball court and lost just to find his ass. This was someone who got better through the many fights and times he was jumped in Baltimore.

Sure Jalen came back, his fists flying, but Lockland didn't give him the chance to breathe. They cheered with every blow. He knew the streets loved a hero, and that person was Lockland.

Jalen swung again, but Lockland caught his wrist, twisting it hard enough to make him scream for Cakes before Lockland sent him flying across the parking lot.

The fight dragged on, each blow heavier than the last. Lockland's knuckles split, but he didn't stop. He hated himself for bringing Memory to that restaurant, only for her to be exposed to nightmares due to the murder Jalen committed right before her eyes.

He had to punish the boy.

Jalen's lip was bleeding, his eye swelling shut, but he kept coming, refusing to stay down. And then Lockland landed a clean hook to Jalen's jaw, the impact sending him to the ground. His head hit the asphalt with a hollow *thud*, and for a moment, he didn't move.

The lot was silent except for Lockland's heavy breathing, his chest rising and falling as he stood over his brother. The blood on his knuckles dripped onto the ground, mixing with the dirt on his boots.

Jalen moaned, rolling onto his side, but he didn't try to get up. He could take no more.

Lockland looked down at him, his voice steady but cold. "Don't ever let me see you again."

"So this how you treat somebody who looked out for you?" He said grabbing his head for pain relief. "You gonna regret this shit trust me. And when you do I'll be waiting."

Cakes' needles clicked softly, the yarn gliding through her steady hands as she knitted. The red scarf she worked on was thick, made of mismatched scraps of fabric and yarn she was trying to weave into something beautiful.

The thing was, she kept forgetting what she was doing throughout the process and added new patches to avoid whatever was happening in her mind. She always knitted when life was heavy.

After hearing Memory's story again, Lockland paced back and forth across the living room, his boots tapping against the worn wooden floor. Every now and then, he'd glance toward the bloody coat by the front door, the red stain already dark and crusting over.

Memory sat on a pillow on the floor, her knees pulled up to her chest. She hugged her legs tight, her face pressed against them like she could hide from the world if she tried hard enough. She hadn't said anything since she told her mother what happened, but it would keep her up many a night.

In the kitchen, Turner rifled through the fridge, the old door creaking as he leaned in, the sound of glass jars and can goods knocking as he stuffed what he could into the deep pockets of his coat.

Cakes still didn't look up from her knitting. She didn't need to. Her voice was calm, but there was a sharpness to it that cut through the room like a blade.

"After this," she said, her needles still clicking, "we can all agree that Jalen is never to come back to this house again. Now normally I wouldn't feel the need to say such things," she looked at Lockland, "But it's obvious my requests are falling on dead ass ears."

Lockland stopped pacing, his back straightening. "I'm sorry, ma."

Cakes' eyes flicked up, just for a moment, toward the bloody coat by the door. It sat there like it belonged to someone else...like a piece of Jalen still haunted the house. None of them had bothered to move it, as if picking it up would make the night real all over again.

"You sure about that?" She asked him.

Lockland finally spoke. “I don’t want nothin’ to do with him and I will never disobey you or break a promise again. So he will never, ever, come back in this house or any house you own.”

“He said he could have me,” Memory whispered remembering the words the whistler said. “Why he say that, Lock?”

“It don’t matter,” Cakes said. “He’s gone.”

“I don’t wanna see him no more either,” Memory whispered.

In the kitchen, Turner shut the fridge with his elbow, a few cans clinking in his pockets as he walked back into the room. “Doesn’t much matter to me,” he said, shrugging like it was nothing. “Ain’t like he gonna listen anyway. Jalen’s gone, been gone.” He snorted, pulling his coat tighter around him as if he was of the highest caliber. “Besides, y’all wouldn’t let me stay so why should anything be different for a criminal?”

“Good...he said he’s a ghost...so let him stay dead.” Cakes’ needles stopped as she looked up at her family before focusing on Lockland. “Don’t let your heart get in the way, because he will eat it just to see you die.”

Lockland couldn't take it anymore. He turned on his heel and started toward the hallway, but Turner stepped in front of him, blocking the door.

"Wait," Turner said.

Lockland stared at him, his shoulders tense. "What?"

Turner looked him up and down for a second, his usual cocky grin nowhere to be found. "You know why he did it right?"

"Nah."

Turner licked his dry lips and leaned in closer, his voice still quiet. His breath smelling of vinegar. "That man," he jerked his head toward the bloody coat, "is the one who raped him a year ago today."

Lockland's chest tightened. "Wait...what?"

"A year ago. Same day." Turner's voice cracked a little, like the words hurt coming out. "I didn't tell nobody 'cause it didn't matter because for whatever reason, when ma put him out, he went back to the van man for money. Guess Jalen hated himself for it. So he had to kill his ass."

"So that's what happened the day he took him in the van?"

"Hell no...Jalen had been violated by that man long before the van took him. It's when he kidnapped him and wouldn't let him go, and let his friends get in on it too, that fucked up his life."

Lockland blinked, his body suddenly feeling too heavy for the room. His heart pounded in his ears, drowning out the sound of the ticking clock on the wall. "Why didn't you say nothin'?" He whispered, his voice barely there.

Turner shrugged again, but this time it wasn't smug. "You think anybody cared back then? Jalen was a fuck up. And don't pretend you weren't happy when ma put him out. You had her all to yourself. Face in the titties ass nigga."

Lockland's stomach twisted, his thoughts a mess. It was easier to be mad at Jalen, *so much easier*, than to think about what had really gone down. But now it made sense.

All of it.

CHAPTER ONE

TEN YEARS LATER - 2024

Today felt like a good day...or at least it started that way.

Lockland Logan, sometimes called *Locked and Loaded* because he kept his hand on a trigger, stood behind his mother, brushing her thinning gray hair with care. She sat in her favorite chair by the open window, the once-vibrant garden outside now overgrown and neglected. The scent of banana candles wafted through the room, which was her favorite smell, something that always brought her a small slice of peace.

Snooze by *Sza* played on her speaker.

The brush moved slowly through her hair, its bristles catching on knots that Lockland carefully worked out, his large hands surprisingly gentle. Cakes closed her eyes, letting the steady rhythm soothe her.

Lockland didn't say much.

He rarely did when he was with her. It was enough to just be here, to feel like things were okay, even if just for a moment.

As he went to work, his tattooed neck peeked from the collar of his leather jacket, the ink snaking down his arms and disappearing under the blue jean fabric of his pants. Per usual, cold or not, he wore no shirt beneath the jacket, his bare chest catching the gleam of the silver diamond chain hanging around his neck. It sparkled as he moved his muscles which flexed with the slightest of motions.

Although he was used to dealing with more heavy weighted matters, for the moment he worked quietly, tying her hair into a loose bun. In his mind this should have been Memory's job, but his younger sister was trash and too consumed by her boyfriend Davis to spend time helping their ailing mother. Lockland exhaled sharply through his nose at the thought, his irritation simmering beneath the surface.

"Lockland," she whispered.

He froze for a moment, frowning as the sound settled in his ears. Calling him by his name was not normal although it should have been. She was so out of it at times that she would often call him anything but a child of God.

Weird things often went down in that bedroom lately that always put him on edge. Dementia, FTD to be exact, had taken most of the good moments, and replaced them with nightmares.

"Lockland," she repeated.

Quickly, he forced a smile and walked around to face her. "What up, ma?"

"I know I lean on you a lot," she began, her voice carrying the slight tremor of her illness, "but I'm gonna need to lean on you a bit more, son." She scratched the raised scar on her face from the glass all those years back, which threatened, unsuccessfully, to steal her beauty.

Lockland backed away a step, still close enough to feel the warmth of her presence. "I'm listening," he said, a knot forming in his chest.

"It's almost time."

"Ma, stop talking like that. You—."

"Listen to me, boy. While my mind is right."

He nodded.

"I never told you this, but I knew this day would come. My mama had dementia and so when she started forgetting, I knew I would too. It's one of the reasons I named my only daughter Memory and the reason I chose you over Jalen."

He took a deep breath. "What you saying, ma? Get to it because you scaring me."

"I need three things from you."

Dragging tattooed hands down his face, he scratched at his bare chest before crossing his arms. "Line 'em up."

She took a deep breath, her frail hands resting on the arms of her chair. "When I go on, I need you to take care of Memory."

"Ma, you know she don't listen to me. She eighteen and that nigga be gassing her up with—"

"I need you to take care of her anyway," she said firmly. "If she don't act right, force it! Don't act like you don't force other things that you want." She paused. "Anyways, with that boy she got trouble, and I don't want the streets to have her, son. Please."

Lockland's jaw tightened, his frustration threatening to bubble over. But he nodded. "What else, ma?"

"Also," she continued, her voice softening, "I need you to keep working on what I taught you. You know...the sewing. It'll come in handy at some point."

"Come on, ma," he said, shaking his head. "You know sewing ain't my thing. I did it to help you but—."

"Isn't cool enough for you. Is that it?"

He sighed.

"That skill you find so soft was taught to me by my daddy. And you're even better at it than him. Let's not even forget that the skill has taken care of this family for years."

Lockland sighed, following her gaze to the sewing stand in the corner of the room. It resembled a body with no limbs. It was tattered, its surface worn from generations of use. Her great-great-grandmother on her daddy's side had passed it down, and it was now hers. The thought of it one day being his, left a weight he wasn't sure he could bare. Afterall, he wasn't a legacy type of nigga.

"I want you to use that," she whispered. "Keep it with you...and cherish it always."

He took another deep breath. "Okay, ma. What else?"

Her expression turned serious, the air in the room growing heavier. "Before you bury me...and I need you to hear me good on this...deal with every evil thing you have on the streets. And I mean everyone. I want you to let it go before you put me in the ground, or I won't rest in peace."

"I'm not even out here like that anymore."

"I know about what you wanna do, Lockland. And you have my blessing," She paused. "But do it all before you bury me and then let it go. Or my soul won't rest."

This sent him over the edge.

Did she know the man he wanted to kill was Jalen?

Anyway she was tripping. She knew full well he was a street nigga. And that things couldn't be packaged and cleaned up so easily. At the same time she was certain that if he said yes, he would never lie to her.

"What is your answer?"

"Ma—."

"Do you promise or not?"

"I promise."

She breathed deeply while he found no comfort in their newfound arrangement. "You got all this energy for me, but what about your oldest son? Huh? After all these years he still out here getting high and—"

"Don't you worry none about Turner," she said, her tone unwavering. "Everyone...and I do mean everyone...pays what they owe. Even you."

Fuck was that supposed to mean?

A loud noise shattered the moment, echoing from the living room. Lockland stiffened, his instincts kicking in. Without a word, he moved toward the sound, detouring to grab his gun from the side table where it rested. Normally it was glued on his hip, but this was his mama's house and so a strap needed its place far away from his mother's head which he just finished brushing.

Bending the corner, in the living room, he softened slightly at the sight of his brother Turner, though his irritation was quick to return. Turner stood hunched over, his clothes soiled and wrinkled, reeking of sweat and stale cigarettes.

"I need mama," Turner said, his voice sounded as if he hadn't drunk water in months.

Lockland knew that look and wanted him to kick rocks asap.

"You not getting ma," Lockland replied flatly. "So go that way," he added, pointing toward the door.

"Mama!" Turner yelled over his shoulder. "Lockland won't let me see you! I gotta lay eyes on you to make sure you taken care of."

"Taken care of. How you sound? You don't give a fuck about her well-being. Never have!"

"Ma, are you okay back there? Or do I gotta call the police?"

"I said get out of here before I drop your ass. I'm not playing with you."

"Mama! Mama!" He continued to yell. Just the sound of him begging like a kid had him wanting to crack open his skull.

"Leave before I—."

"Let him in," Cakes' voice called from the other room.

Lockland took a deep breath, his jaw tightening as he waved his brother through. He didn't need to ask what Turner wanted. It was always the same.

Money.

Turner smirked, bumped him to the right and bopped toward the back. It was no need in following him. He would win regardless.

"Don't give it to him, ma," Lockland said, his voice a warning as he leaned against the wall and scratched his chest.

But it was already too late.

Turner emerged moments later, stuffing fifty dollars into his pocket with a self-satisfied grin.

"What pill you gonna pop now?"

"Whatever pill I want to nigga," he admitted. "Fuck difference do it make to you? You wanted her, you got her. Be grateful because we all know she loves you more than all our asses put together."

Lockland watched him leave, the screen door slamming repeatedly on its hinges as it swung back and forth.

"See you later," Carl the Stump called from the porch.

"Fuck out my face," Turner said as he slithered out of sight.

Suddenly Carl yelled, "Whoa, man! Whoa, man!"

Lockland peeped out the door, left and right before looking down at him.

When he was done yelling, the old blind man puffed on his sweet cigar, the fragrant smoke curling into the night air. Despite his lack of sight, Carl knew everything that went on in Cakes' house. His presence was a quiet, steady reminder of the neighborhood's history and its secrets.

Lockland wasn't even fully sure why his mother let him back in her life. But when he appeared at the doorstep of her new house a few years back, Lockland realized he had special skills and decided to keep him around. Plus if the rumor was true, he was Jalen's father.

Lockland closed the door and returned to his mother. "I can't stand him," he admitted. "I hope you don't try to make me promise nothing about him cause—."

"Nah, things will work its own way out with your brother."

"How you so sure?"

"You look at a man's actions...but sometimes its deeper than that. Like I said, sooner or later, we all pay what we owe. Trust, Turner is miserable and paying for his now. But he ain't done paying." She took a deep breath. "Shit...neither am I."

CHAPTER TWO

Freshly showered, Lockland stepped out his room, the scent of soap and aftershave clinging to him. Next he removed his foldable velvet lint brush and wiped imaginary lint off his jeans. It was more of a habit than anything else. Moving toward the door he grabbed his cell phone off the side table and made a call.

"Any news on Jalen, man?"

"You know if I had news I would tell you," Wakes said. "On second thought I probably would come past your mama's crib because I know how important it is."

"I need you to find him, man," Lockland admitted. "We gotta find him like yesterday."

"Well, let a nigga move."

With his phone in his pocket he tugged the front door open. The early evening air was thick, and the distant aroma of barbecue smoke filled the atmosphere. He handed an orange to Carl, who was perched on the porch as always, puffing on a sweet cigar.

"Thank you kindly," Carl said, his lips curling into a knowing grin.

Lockland tilted his head. “I still don’t understand how you be knowing it’s me.”

Carl chuckled, a deep sound that vibrated in his chest. “That part is easy. You never forget me.” He smashed the cigar out and went to peeling the orange. “Although I will say you not gonna like what you see next.”

Not knowing what he meant, Lockland shook his head, as he descended the porch steps. Despite wearing a black jacket and being shirtless, a crisp white T-shirt draped loosely over his chest, and his designer jeans were cinched by a Gucci belt. His black Impala gleamed in the driveway under the streetlights, but his attention was immediately drawn to the beat-up red Civic parked behind it.

“Hold up, I know her ass not crazy.”

Frowning, Lockland moved closer and saw his 18-year-old sister, Memory, perched on Davis’ lap in the driver’s seat. She was moving up and down like a wave and he suddenly felt ill.

Was this bitch fuckin’ in the wild?

Already he was regretting his promise to Cakes.

His killer instincts flared and without hesitation, he swung the driver’s side door open and pulled her out. Davis’ dick glistened due to being wet as he fought desperately to tuck it back inside.

Memory's gold locs tumbled down her shoulders, and her light brown skin flushed with embarrassment and anger as her brother gripped her by both arms and slammed her against the already dented car.

"Why the fuck you out here being fast?" He roared. "You really fucking this nigga outside your mama's house?"

Before Memory could respond, Davis emerged from the car, his oversized jeans slightly unbuttoned. His red cap was turned backward, and he moved with the false confidence of someone who thought faking tough was enough, despite his short stature.

"I don't see why it's a problem," Davis said, his tone casual but laced with defiance. "Memory old enough to get what she want. And what she want is this D."

Lockland's eyes narrowed as he let her go, gripped him by the collar and stole him in the lips. His mouth flooded with blood and in an instant the ego was snatched from his chest. Lockland wasn't just anyone. He was a man with a reputation...a deadly one at that.

Davis retreated in his rat hole, feet planted on the ground as he whispered words of anger under his breath while sucking back blood.

"Why you hit him? You ain't—."

"Shut the fuck up!" He pointed in her face. "I don't need you out here being a hoe," he said firmly. "If mama saw you—"

"But mama don't see me now do she?" Spit flew from her mouth, dampening his jacket. "Or have you forgotten she doesn't remember any fucking thing!" Her voice cracked with anger and pain. "Plus she be on these streets fucking more people than me. So please don't act like—"

The slap came before Lockland could stop himself. The sound of his palm meeting her cheek echoed out through the night. Memory's face snapped to the side, her locs falling forward like a curtain. The moment it happened, regret flooded through his heart.

"I'm sorry, little sis," he whispered as he tried to hold her. "I was just—"

But Davis, ever the opportunist, was already out of the car, with tissue pressed against his swelling lip. "You done enough," he said as he stepped between them. "Take your position, babe."

She didn't hesitate. Without a word, she climbed into the passenger seat, her face turned away from Lockland. Davis slid back into the driver's seat, as the engine coughed and hacked like it had Covid. The Civic sputtered to life and ticked down the road, its taillights disappearing into the night.

Lockland stood frozen, the guilt of his actions rooting him in place.

Shannon pulled into the driveway of her house, just three blocks over from the Logan residence. The engine fell silent, leaving only the faint chirp of crickets and the distant hum of traffic in the air. She sat for a moment, gripping the steering wheel tightly. She had just finished a grueling shift at the grocery store, and all she wanted was to step inside, crack open the half-empty bottle of vodka in her bag, and drown out the memories that haunted her every night.

But there was a problem. The backseat was filled with grocery bags...heavy, overstuffed, and screaming for attention she didn't have the energy to give. She sighed, letting her head fall back against the headrest before grabbing the vodka and guzzling it all.

And then motion caught her eye.

It was Lockland.

He had parked haphazardly in front of her house and was already making his way toward her. Shannon's sigh deepened as she stuffed the liquid shame back and attempted to muster the strength to grab the bags.

She knew better.

He would never let her do it herself.

"Let me get that up off you," Lockland said, his voice firm but calm as he reached for the bags.

"When you gonna leave me alone?" She asked.

"I told you," he said, his eyes meeting hers with quiet determination. "For the rest of my life, I'm gonna look after you. And I know that ain't what you wanna hear but it's the truth."

"We not together anymore, Lockland."

"I know," he replied softly. "And I'm sorry about that."

His sincerity stole whatever fight she had left. Shannon let him take the bags, her arms falling limp at her sides. Together, they walked toward her front door as the smell of the freshly cut lawn with its neat edges filled the air. Lockland's silent care was everywhere, even in the details she wished she could ignore.

Inside, she dropped onto the worn couch, the cushions swallowing her whole. Lockland carried the bags to the kitchen, unloading each item with precision. The rhythmic clink of jars and the rustle of plastic filled the quiet house as he put everything in its proper place.

When he was finished, he returned to the living room and took a quick glance around. Magazines were scattered across the coffee table, an empty glass hung on the edge, and the faint scent of stale smoky air lingered.

No use in complaining.

Lockland set to work, tidying up with practiced efficiency. He straightened the magazines, washed the glass, and opened a window to let in the cool evening breeze. By the time he was done, the room felt fresher, lighter.

Next, he extended a hand toward her.

"I'm good, Lock."

"Please…let me do this."

Shannon didn't argue. She let him help her to her feet and into her bedroom.

Once inside, Lockland assisted her in removing her shoes, kissing the top of both of her feet. Next he helped remove her clothing and she sat naked before he wrapped her in the thick lavender robe with the duck faces throughout.

She didn't protest, too tired to fight, and too accustomed to his silent routine of care. He left briefly, returning moments later after a steaming bath was drawn in her honor.

He helped her inside and then paced the floor in the hallway while texting on his phone. Wild thoughts fucking up his life.

Cakes was dying...Cakes was dying.

Where was Jalen's bitch ass?

When she emerged from the bathroom wrapped in the robe, her face softened, and a slight sigh escaped her lips. She had some relief but not much. As always, Lockland took her hand again, guiding her to the bed. He pulled back the covers and waited as she climbed safely inside.

Sitting on the edge, he removed his jeans, leaving on his shorts, and slipped in behind her. His arms wrapped around her like a protective shield, holding her close as she began to weep. The cold chain on her back tensed her for a moment before it warmed between their skin.

Like clockwork, the sobs came quietly at first, then heavier. Lockland held her through it all, his grip steady and his breathing calm. He didn't say a word. He didn't need to.

His presence was enough.

Knowing what she needed, he moved his hand between her soft thighs. Freeing one finger, he slipped it inside of her warm tunnel and stroked it slowly. Her body jittered and jumped but suddenly she was starting to feel something besides emotional pain. The wetter she got, the better she felt until she let out a soft moan.

She was forever putty in his hands, and she hated him for that shit.

Only when her cries finally subsided, her breathing deep and even, did he let go.

Some shit happened that changed them. But when it came to loving a woman next to Cakes, there was no one he loved harder. Slowly, he slipped out of bed, careful not to disturb her. He glanced back once before heading toward the door.

The night outside greeted him with its cool stillness, but Lockland didn't stop to take it in. There was still more of his day left to handle.

Lockland stepped into the homeless shelter, the overpowering scent of cleaning supplies and simmering soup wafting through the air. He nodded at the receptionist, Jessica, who perked up the moment she spotted his bare chest and that leather coat.

"Hey, boy," she said, her voice dripping with playful flirtation. "Your fine ass gonna catch a fever if you don't put on a shirt. No worries though...I'll take care of you if I can sit on that face."

She threw the pussy, but he dodged it and said, "What up, Jess."

"She in the back."

Lockland had already given a quick wink and was on his way.

The narrow hallway led him to his play aunt's office. Myra's door was slightly open, her no-nonsense voice carrying into the hall.

She was a force, standing no taller than five feet three but commanding the respect of anyone who crossed her path. She didn't need this job at the shelter. Between her side hustles...selling drugs and running other shadowy enterprises...she was more than capable of taking care of herself. She was not blood related, but she was yet another woman who saw something in Lockland and rose to the challenge to look after him.

Lockland pushed the door open wider and stepped inside. Myra sat behind her desk, her small frame somehow filling the room with her presence. Her eyes glanced up at him as she held the phone to her ear.

"We only need the items on the list, ma'am," Myra said, shaking her head. "Please don't bring mac and cheese up in here. Ain't nobody trying to eat that cat hair flooded shit."

Lockland dropped into the chair across from her. Myra glanced at him briefly, then returned to her call, her tone sharp. "You know what, I'm tired of talking to your ass."

She hung up with a click before leaning back in her chair. "How you doing over there, nephew?" She asked, her eyes narrowing as she studied him.

"You know what it is with me," Lockland replied, his smile fading.

"Jalen."

"Always," he admitted.

"I detect something else." Myra got up from her chair, walked over, and grabbed his hand. She brought his finger to her nose and gave it a quick sniff. Her expression shifted instantly. She smelled the faint but not unpleasant odor of pussy.

"Oh," she said knowingly. "That's what's going on."

"It's not like that," Lockland said quickly, but his words lacked conviction.

"I wish you could let her go," Myra interrupted, folding her arms across her chest. "She done told you time and time again she don't want no hero. Why don't you—."

"I'm gonna need you to stay out my business, auntie," Lockland said, his voice firm but respectful.

"Fair enough," she said, stepping back with a shrug.

"What you got for me?"

She went to her desk and pulled out a key to a safe which she unlocked. Next she removed a small notepad and a lighter. She handed the paper to her nephew. He scanned it and said, "What he do?"

She frowned. "You normally don't wanna know what he did. Just as long as it doesn't involve women, children or squares."

"I'm asking now."

She nodded. "He beat up his son's mother last month and she been having nightmares ever since. According to the woman's father it ain't been the first time. He fears the next time he will kill her."

Lockland grinned because his aunt knew him well.

It was the perfect job.

Focusing on the paper again, he grabbed the lighter and put it to the document. They both watched it go up in flames.

Flames.

For some reason they always excited him.

When it was nothing more than ashes he said, "What about, Jalen? Any word from your connects?" He paused. "Because I've been looking for this dude for almost a year. There's no way he can go missing this long unless he back living on the streets. He too tied into his neighborhood."

"You scare him," Myra laughed, leaning against the edge of her desk. "He not taking a chance."

Lockland clenched his jaw, frustration simmering beneath the surface. "So what. He's just gonna hide forever?"

"He's waiting," Myra said, her voice calm but firm. "For your deathbed or his."

The block party was alive with chaotic energy, the music pounding from oversized speakers, the voices of the crowd rising and falling in waves. Children darted between clusters of adults, their laughter piercing through the hum of conversations. The smell of grilled meat, beer, and fried food hung thick in the air, along with the stank of cigarette smoke.

This is what Lockland did for money.

This is what he always did for money when Big Boy and them found out he was good on the streets. And he had gotten so good that if you were on his list, you could consider yourself gone.

Low key he was starting to wonder if it was all hype though, because after what Jalen did to him a year ago, he had yet to get his revenge.

Suddenly a man stumbled into the party, clutching a red plastic cup that sloshed with every unsteady step. His shirt was untucked and stained as he weaved through the crowd like a pinball, spilling liquor on unsuspecting people trying to enjoy a good time.

"Watch it, man!" Someone shouted as the cup tipped again, beer splattering onto their shirt.

"Sorry!" The man slurred, his words heavy and indistinct. His demeanor that of someone who had long passed the point of sobriety.

But he wasn't any man.

The partygoers shot him dirty looks but quickly dismissed him as just another drunk who had done the most. He continued to stagger through the crowd, his cup now nearly empty, his shoulders slumping forward as he approached the hotdog stand.

And that's where Lockland found him.

Donny, with a yellow grease-stained apron tied around his waist, flipping sausages on the grill with a pair of worn tongs. "Hotdogs! Get your hotdogs! Best on the block!"

Cap.

As if he called his name, the drunk stumbled up to the stand, his red cup dangling loosely from his fingers. He slammed it down on the counter, spilling what little remained of the liquid across the surface. Donny's eyes flicked to the mess, his expression darkening.

"Fuck is you doing?" Donny yelled, his voice shrieking. "You messing my shit up!"

The man let out a soft laugh, swaying slightly on his feet. He reached into his pocket with fumbling fingers, pulling out a crumpled, wet twenty-dollar bill. “Hotdog. Let me...let me get one up off you,” he said, before burping.

Donny stared at the bill in disgust. “You gotta be kidding me.”

“You want the money...you want...you want...it or not?”

The man’s head bobbed up and down, his glazed eyes fixed. Donny turned away and grabbed a hotdog bun as he moved toward the grill. He had plans to take the whole twenty for his troubles.

The moment Donny’s back was turned, the man straightened slightly, his movements suddenly sharper, more deliberate. In one swift motion, he stepped around the counter, his hand moving with the precision of someone who had done this before.

The blade was small, unassuming, but its presence was lethal. It slipped into Donny’s side with the practiced ease of a prisoner in the yard. The handle pressing against his ribs as the man leaned in close, his voice a low whisper. Next he moved around the back and shanked him several times until he fell over.

If people didn't know they would think they were lovers or partners.

But who would notice? His dogs were trash, and word had gotten around so not many people stopped at his stand anyway.

The commotion of the party continued unabated around them, the music pounding, the people laughing.

With the same staggering gait, Lockland turned and melted back into the crowd.

CHAPTER THREE

The ambulance sat in the obscurely lit parking lot of a closed-down restaurant called Cracker Bread. The pavement beneath it was littered with shards of broken glass and stray wrappers, remnants of a once-busy spot now abandoned to time. The ambulance, with its faded paint and dented exterior, seemed unassuming, but it held secrets.

Inside, the vehicle had been transformed into a compact yet luxurious mobile home. The spot was remarkably well-organized...a small sink, a stove, and a tiny shower shared space with the cramped bathroom.

Jalen had gotten the idea from the trend on YouTube of ambulances being turned into mobile homes and he figured it would be an easy way to avoid detection. And it worked too. Because although he had to give up his luxurious lifestyle, he successfully evaded Lockland for a year.

But not everything was sweet.

Jalen had a secret.

One that only he and his friends knew about.

The small bathroom inside the ambulance reeked of stomach acid and old sweat, the kind of smell that clung to the walls no matter how many windows were cracked open. Jalen hunched over the tiny sink, his hands gripping the sides hard enough to make his knuckles pop. His face was sweaty and the veins in his neck bulged as another wave of nausea hit him.

He gagged, his body convulsing, and bile splashed into the sink with a wet *splatter*. The sound echoed in the confined area. His throat burned, raw and scraped from forcing himself to throw up. When it was over, he coughed, spitting the last remnants into the stained basin. The mirror in front of him was cracked, but it didn't matter. He already knew what he'd see.

Jalen's teeth were yellowed and uneven, the enamel worn down from years of purging. His gums bled when he brushed too hard, and he couldn't remember the last time he'd smiled without pressing his lips together to hide the damage. He wiped his mouth with the back of his hand, staring at his reflection with hollow eyes.

Outside the bathroom, Tink and Everett were waiting, their low whispers blending with the hum of the ambulance's engine. Thanks to Jalen's dope game, they all had a baby come up, which included fresh cuts, new clothes and clean boxers, although not everybody took advantage of those honors.

"You think he's okay?" Tink asked, his voice hesitant.

"When is he ever okay?"

The door creaked open, and Jalen stepped out, his shoulders slumped and his face glistening with sweat. The rancid smell that followed him like a shadow, hit Tink and Everett in the face like a wall.

"Damn, J!" Everett coughed, waving a hand in front of his nose. "Fuck is you doing, man?" He stepped forward, grabbed the door, and slammed it shut before the stench could spread further.

Jalen sat on the edge of the bed, a cigarette balanced between his fingers, its ash threatening to fall. He scratched at his low-cut hair, his bloodshot eyes half open from throwing up and the substance he'd taken earlier.

But he was growing agitated.

The streets were starting to rumble. Claiming he was soft and scared to let Lockland see him. And for the most part they were right.

"Where my girl at?" Jalen asked, exhaling a plume of smoke that curled upward. "She ain't coming?"

They both shook their heads no.

"She ain't trynna fuck a nigga in a box huh?" He paused. "Give her some money for her rent...nah give her half and tell her to come see me for the rest."

"Stop fucking with them upscale hoes," Tink replied from the makeshift dining area. His lanky frame leaned back against the wall, one leg stretched out, the other bent as he twirled a knife between his fingers.

"I can't do that," he said honestly. "She the one."

Tink waved the air. "Fuck all that...if you want out of this box to go get your bitch, you need to hit Lockland where he breathes. I mean, people saying you scared of a man who's just that...a fucking man. He bleeds like anybody else."

"That's your problem," Everett interjected, shaking his head. His muscular body filled the tiny space, as he leaned forward on the counter. "You always trying to reduce a nigga to one level when all men aren't the same. That's the reason Jalen's living in this bitch. And unless he wants to die a quick death, I suggest he stays right here."

"Until how long?" Tink shot back, his impatience clear. "We don't got no more say so on the blocks."

"That's not true," Everett said. "Niggas still know what it is." He focused on Jalen. "Don't let this man talk you off no cliff because he impatient. Let's let what I got cooking work its way through."

Jalen's tired gaze flicked to Everett. The tension was broken by a sharp knock. Their hands hovered above their guns, muscles tense, eyes darting toward the small window near the top of the door.

"It's your brother," Everett responded, squinting as he peered through the window.

Jalen smirked. "Let him in."

The door creaked open, and Turner stumbled inside, his head almost slamming into the steering wheel because he couldn't lift it up. Once settled, they took in the stench of cheap liquor.

"What took you so long?" Everett asked. "I thought you were coming earlier because I better not discover you playing both sides."

Jalen didn't need to say it out loud, but he was always one second away from ending Turner's life. The only reason Turner was still breathing was his occasional usefulness. At the end of the day he sometimes knew where Lockland rested his head when he wasn't at Cakes' although getting to Lockland was easier said than done.

The Dust Boys always kept eyes on the man.

"Like I said on the phone, I'm here with some info you could use," Turner slurred, swaying slightly as he spoke.

"I'm listening," Jalen replied, leaning back against the bedframe. His cigarette burned down to the filter as he flicked it into a small ashtray.

"Lockland just made ma a promise."

Jalen looked at his men and all fell out laughing.

And then Jalen glared. "Hey, man, put this nigga out of his misery."

Tink reached for his gun when Turner yelled, "I'm serious! She made him promise that before he buries her, he gotta end all beef in the streets."

"Again...what the fuck I care about him making a promise to your mother?" Jalen leaned forward, his stare cutting deep.

"She your mother too," Turner began.

"You and me both know that bitch don't mean nothing to me."

Out of reflex, Turner lunged for him, but Tink moved toward him with an aggressive step. Before he could close the gap, Jalen raised a hand, and Everett followed suit, stopping Tink in his tracks.

Turner raised his hands, a gesture of uneasy peace. “I’m just saying, when it comes to ma, that nigga serious. If he made her a promise that he’s gonna end all beefs before she’s buried, then that’s a promise he intends on keeping. That means he’s gonna leave you be.”

“How come you don’t just kill his ass and get the stacks I got put up for you?”

Turner looked down. “Because I can’t do that. I told you that before.”

“So if he intends on getting out the game when she dies, maybe I can help facilitate that,” Jalen responded, his voice dripping with something dark and unspoken.

Turner’s face hardened, his body stiffening as he sensed the danger in Jalen’s words. “Leave ma out of this,” he said, his voice firmer now.

“I would never,” Jalen replied, the faintest grin playing on his face.

Turner nodded slowly, his gaze shifting between the three men. “Her words were clear...before he buries her, he’ll end all beefs in the streets.”

Jalen's grin widened. "And how's your mother's health looking these days?"

"She ain't been looking too well," Turner admitted, his eyes dropping to the floor. "In my opinion, it's just a matter of time. That's why I'm here."

"Well then," Jalen said, his smile spreading like a serpent's. "I guess I gotta wait."

"Uh...before you do anything," Turner said. "Where my money?"

Jalen didn't feel like waiting...

The night was quiet, the kind of stillness that felt unnatural, as though the world was holding its breath. The faint glow of the streetlights barely illuminated the cracked sidewalk in front of Cakes' house. Tink approached first, his boots crunching softly against the gravel. He carried two bags: one containing a portable wood stove, the other filled with fragrant wood chips.

Jalen followed a few paces behind.

There Carl the stump was...sitting.

He was always fucking there.

With that nose that could smell a nigga a mile away.

Tink knelt on the lawn in front of the house, placing the stove carefully on the ground. The metal gleamed faintly under the pale moonlight. He opened the bag of wood chips and packed them into the stove. With a practiced flick of his lighter, a small flame burst to life, licking hungrily at the chips. Smoke began to curl upward, thick and fragrant, spreading quickly as the fire consumed its fuel.

Carl, his sightless eyes staring into the distance, sniffed the air, his face twisting in confusion. "Who's there?" He sniffed again, his head tilting slightly, his ears straining for sounds that didn't belong. "I know you out there! Who are you?"

Tink didn't answer.

He watched the smoke rise, the scent of burning wood chips creating a thick, aromatic barrier. The old man's keen sense of smell would be dulled, his ability to distinguish scents muted by the overpowering odor.

Satisfied, Jalen slipped around the side of the house, moving like a shadow. He reached the backdoor, cracked the glass and was about to enter when he heard Cakes' soft humming voice. Within seconds, wearing an ice blue housecoat, her frail frame appeared in the low light filtering in from the kitchen. She clutched the railing for support, her steps slow but steady.

Damn. She had lost a lot of weight. And a lot of appeal. He was about to kill her quick, but for a second familiarity ran rampant in his mind.

Nah, he couldn't be soft.

If her death would bring him freedom from Lockland he would have to take the chance. Whether she was his mother or not.

Jalen crept forward.

His hand moved to his pocket, his fingers brushing against the cold steel of his blade. He waited until she reached the bottom step. She was almost in his grasp. But suddenly the shuffle of footsteps behind him stopped his murder plans.

"Who's there?" Carl called out again, his voice closer this time. The old man had moved, his instincts pushing him toward the back of the house despite the smoke that clouded his senses. "Cakes, is that you? Something's wrong. I can feel it."

Silence.

"Cakes, you ain't out the house are you?"

Cakes turned toward the sound, her frail silhouette outlined by the light spilling from the kitchen window. "Leave me alone, nigga, damn! You can't have no more pussy!"

She took off running.

Jalen was incensed. He made a move to chase her, but the neighbors had started to come out, all wondering what was up with the portable wood burning stove in front of Cakes' house.

Jalen's jaw tightened, frustration flashing in his dark eyes.

As if he could see, Carl moved closer, his hands outstretched as he navigated the yard. Just then Jalen stepped a bit close, and the old man froze, his head tilting slightly as he sniffed the air. The scent of the burning wood chips still hung thick, masking Jalen's true presence.

But who needed scents when he could hear his words. "You'll pay for this."

Carl flinched but then calmed down. "There you are...I know exactly who I'm dealing with now."

CHAPTER FOUR

After taking care of Donny, Lockland was on some other shit.

And so he crept down the street in his Impala, his eyes scanning every corner, every shadow, for a sign of Jalen. He navigated his stomping grounds, knowing Jalen loved the limelight more than he would admit.

Nothing.

As he turned toward the even darker part of Baltimore, a loud sound pierced the tense silence inside the car. Ordinarily he didn't like a ringing phone but with his mother being sick he had to be prepared.

"What up, sis? You good?" He asked, keeping his eyes on the road.

"Lock!" Memory screamed, her voice frantic. "I can't find mama!"

Lockland slammed the brakes, causing the car behind him to screech to a halt, its horn blaring angrily. His heart thudded in his chest as he gripped the wheel. "What you mean you can't find ma?" He barked, his voice booming.

"I went...I went....out with Davis," Memory stuttered. Whenever she lied, she did the same thing, which was a tell-tale sign that something was off.

"So basically, you left ma by herself while you were keeping time with a bum. When I see that nigga I'ma kill him. You tell him that too!" Lockland snapped, spinning the wheel into a hard U-turn. The tires squealed as he cut across oncoming traffic, earning more horn play.

He didn't give a fuck though.

Memory's voice continued on the line, filled with excuses, but he paid her no mind. Her words were background noise as the fifteen-minute drive took him five.

Once outside Lockland parked haphazardly on the sidewalk. He noticed a wood smoker but didn't understand the placement on his mother's front lawn. Barely throwing the car into park, he bolted through the front door where he found Memory on the couch, her face buried in her hands as she cried.

"Tell me everything you remember," he demanded, his voice cutting through her sobs.

"Like...like...I went...because...Davis wanted to show me something for five minutes. It wasn't that long. I promise."

"I don't give a fuck about you smashing that nigga right now! Fuck was ma wearing?"

Memory looked up, her tear-streaked face trembling. "She had on the ice blue housecoat. The one she always wears."

Lockland didn't wait for her to say more.

He hit it toward the back of the house, his heart pounding. The backyard grass and brush crackled under his boots as he ran to search for her on foot.

It felt like hours, though it had only been minutes, when a familiar voice broke through his panic. "She's in here!"

He turned to see Cora, a neighbor from down the block, waving frantically in his direction. Relief flooded him, as he rushed into Cora's house. Once inside, he saw his mother standing in the middle of the living room, her housecoat soaked in urine and yellow-green feces.

She looked lost, fragile, and utterly disconnected.

"Thank you. I appreciate this," he said, his voice strained as he fought back his emotions.

"You good, ma?" He checked her briefly for any bruises.

"Don't thank me. But y'all gotta do better about taking care of Cakes. It ain't right. She took care of all y'all."

The words hung in the air, sharp and pointed but he already felt bad.

"Now come give me some love."

This the part that he hated about Cora. She would use any excuse to kiss him open mouthed, talking about that's how the old folk do. Walking up to her he pecked her lips and got out of dodge.

Taking his mother gently by the arm down the block, he led her out of the house and back toward their own. Her movements were hesitant, her eyes darting around at everything.

"Who are you?" She asked him suddenly, her voice trembling. "Get off me!"

"It's me, ma," he said as people watched the two from a distance, each judging with their eyes.

"I don't know you, nigga!" She proceeded to fight him, forcing Lockland to pick her up, the smell of feces and urine mixing with his clothing. "You ain't my son! You ain't my son! I got two boys and you ain't one!"

As Lockland carried her, and she continued to beat him about the face, neck, chest and legs, his heart ached. The blows weren't hard, but they stung in a way that went far deeper. He knew this wasn't her. But knowing didn't make it hurt any less.

When he reached home Carl the stump walked up to him as he continued to fight to get Ms. Cakes inside. The man's message was simple. "He was here."

"You mean—."

"You know exactly what I mean. And I think he was finna do something to her, but she took off. My eyesight ain't about shit so I couldn't stop her."

Lockland was furious.

But there would be plenty of time for revenge later. For now he had to deal with his mother, and it would only get worse.

Much worse.

Lockland had what he called a *one room what not* on the outskirts of town, but he often stayed at Cakes'.

He had a room there, but he wished he didn't when one night he woke up to a warm body and large breasts against his lips. Not only was the body moving up and down, but it was also stroking his dick.

Stiffening, and thinking he was having a wet dream, he was sick when he jumped up and realized what was happening.

Cakes had not only touched him but was attempting to pull his penis out of his pants.

Devastated he popped up and, vomited at the thought of it all. From that moment forward he said he would never stay at night, no matter how much he wanted to watch over her. Dealing with that level of forgetfulness and horniness was tough on Lockland and was high key making him mad.

Concerned by her actions, he took her for help. The doctor told him that FTD dementia could cause hypersexuality and there was no cure, except death.

Again, where was Memory? Why wasn't she more instrumental in all of this?

Six more days passed and there was no relief.

She not only forgot the names of her own children, but she became violent, lashing out whenever they crossed her path. One night, he found her standing in the middle of the living room bucket naked and clutching a knife. Her trembling hands was steady with the blade, daring anyone to come near.

Only he was brave enough and when he did, she soiled herself again. Shit and piss running down her leg and onto the floorboards.

And so, he did what only a son could do. He bathed her, fed her, her favorite soup, and put her to bed. He took the verbal abuse and the occasional slap, knowing the woman who raised him was gone.

It was all on him.

One day, as he prepared her favorite soup, he heard an indistinct sound from the other room. Rushing in, he found her clutching her chest, her breathing shallow and labored. Panic surged through him as he scooped her into his arms, the warmth of her frail body burning into his skin.

There was no time for an ambulance.

Nah.

Instead, Lockland carried her out to his Impala, laying her gently in the passenger seat before slamming the door shut. The engine roared to life when he slipped inside, and the tires screeched as he sped toward the hospital.

CHAPTER FIVE

On a rainy fall day, Cakes passed away.

The sound of raindrops tapping against the hospital window blended with the soft hum of machines, marked the end of her life. Lockland sat at her side, holding her frail hand, the warmth of her touch already fading.

Lockland was stunned.

He knew she had to go but now seemed like too soon.

Pain, regret, and a profound sense of loss churned within him, yet not a single tear fell. There were so many things he wished he could say, so many moments he had dreamed his mother would witness...like the first time he might seriously consider making a woman his wife. Now, those dreams would never leave his mind, forever unrealized.

Yes, he would honor the promises.

To care for his sister Memory, to continue the craft of tailoring and to leave the streets behind before he buried her.

But she wasn't in the grave yet.

He had time.

When he left the hospital, the cold wind stung, including the fact that he made several calls to his siblings to let them know Ms. Cakes was gone. Predictably, neither of them answered the phone. Not a one. He decided to head to her house, needing the comfort of familiarity.

But when Lockland arrived, the sight that greeted him stopped him in his tracks. The front door was open, swinging wildly in the wind. A bad feeling settled, so he released his gun from his hip and stepped inside. The smell of damp wood sent him on another level of rage.

The house was a wreck.

Furniture was overturned, drawers had been pulled out and emptied onto the floor, and shards of glass from a broken lamp littered the carpet. His heart sank when he realized that all the valuables were gone. Not only did they go through the closet of the room he stayed inside from time to time, but they had been through Memory's room too.

The most devastating loss, though, was the sewing stand. The centerpiece of his mother's craft, her legacy, had been taken.

This felt personal.

The sun beat down hard, reflecting off the shiny black surface of the Mercedes parked in Breanna's driveway. The short light skin girl wore jean shorts and a crop top along with her long red fur coat as she held a soapy sponge in one hand and a hose in the other. The smell of car wax and water lingered in the frigid air, her sleek black ponytail swaying with every move.

She was almost done when the low rumble of an engine pulled her attention. When she looked up, she saw the beat-up ambulance coming down the street. Her brown eyes immediately rolled to the back of her head.

Jalen, she thought, sucking her teeth. "This nigga working my nervessss."

The ambulance screeched to a stop in front of her house, like somebody needed assistance, its brakes squealing like nails on a chalkboard. The door swung open, and out stepped Tink and Everett, looking as tired as ever. Jalen followed, jumping out quickly, his sneakers slapping against the pavement.

His face was a sweaty mess.

"Breanna!" He called, running up to her like a lost kid.

She sighed heavily, dropping the sponge into the bucket with a loud *splat* as he wrapped his arms around her, chin digging into her collarbone.

"What now, Jalen?" She asked, her tone flat, annoyed.

"My mom," he said, his voice cracking. Fake tears streamed down his face. "She died. Breanna, my mom's gone. I really need you right now, bae. Please."

Breanna froze for half a second, her lips pressed into a thin line. Behind him, Tink and Everett exchanged a look, their faces tight with something between embarrassment and disbelief. They knew the truth.

Jalen didn't care about Cakes.

He didn't care about anybody but Breanna's gold-digging ass.

Just a couple of days ago, he'd tried to kill the woman who gave him birth in her own backyard, but Carl gutted his plans. And now he was beside himself with grief?

Cap!

"Wow," Breanna finally said, her voice calm but cold. "I'm sorry to hear about your loss and shit,

Jalen. Really, I am. But don't be popping up at my house like this."

Her words hit him like a slap, and he peeled himself off her body. "Breanna," he pleaded, his voice trembling. "Please, I—"

"Can you step back some," she cut him off, crossing her arms over her chest. "Your breath reeks and I can't take it right now."

"My bad, I forgot to brush my teeth after hearing the news."

"Well it smells like you brush your teeth through your ass."

Tink laughed and Jalen looked at him and he looked away.

"Anyways, I'm kind of glad you came. You got my money?"

Jalen's jaw tightened, but he nodded, pulling a wad of cash from his pocket. "Yeah, I got it," he shoved it into her hand. "But can we talk? Just for a minute."

She counted the bills quickly, then glanced back at him, unimpressed. "Talk about what?"

"Come inside," he said, his voice almost desperate. "Just...please. My mama, baby. I need you."

Breanna sighed again but followed him, rolling her eyes so hard it hurt. She walked up the steps, high heels clicking the entire way. Once inside she wanted to bounce. The ambulance smelled like old metal and stale air as he climbed onto the cot, laying down with a moan.

She was confused.

Was he in pain or grief? Because he was doing the most.

Breanna stood in the doorway; arms still crossed. "Okay I'm here...what you want, Jalen?"

"Can you...can you rub my dick or somethin'?" He asked.

"What happens if I don't?"

He glared slowly. "Then I think I'ma need my money back, bitch."

When she turned around to leave she saw Tink and Everett blocking the door.

She hesitated, then rolled her shoulders. "Fine," she walked toward him and got on her knees. Using her coat as a cushion, she removed him from his pants and with her warm palm, centered his whole stick in her mouth. He was already hard as a rock.

She licked the sides.

She licked the tip, and she licked everywhere.

He was feeling better with each slurp and knew it was just a matter of time before he bust. The girl was so good and professional, she didn't even seem to care about the odor stemming off his skin.

Jalen sighed, his body tensed under her licks and jerks. "Why don't you like me?" He asked suddenly, his voice breaking. "Why can't you love me, Breanna?"

She pumped harder, stronger and before she knew it, cream oozed through her fingers.

To say the woman was skilled was an understatement. This was why he wanted her so badly. Next to her looks, her fuck game was paramount.

"You really wanna know?" She wiped the nut off her hands and onto his jeans. Next she pulled a stick of gum from her pocket and got to popping.

"I need to know, baby," he whispered. "Whatever you want, I will do."

She rose and leaned down slightly, her breath warm against his ear. "A real man wouldn't be hiding like a rat. A real man wouldn't be running from a nigga who breathe just like he do. Find him, get your penthouse back, and I might take you seriously."

The words sliced through him, sharper than he expected. But he took it as a challenge.

She walked toward the door where Everett and Tink were still waiting. "Can I leave now?"

Tink looked in and Jalen nodded yes, causing her to storm out.

When she was back digging into her bucket, Tink and Everett stepped all the way inside.

"Let's go," he said, his voice flat. "I need a burger and after that, I'ma find out some info on Lockland. I just remembered the perfect place to go."

The bell above the door jingled as Jalen pushed into the small corner store, the scent of spices, old wood, and mold hitting him immediately. The place was dismal, the fluorescent lights buzzed intently, and the shelves were stacked high with canned goods, bags of rice, and snacks that had probably been sitting there too long.

Behind the counter, an old man sat on a stool, his face wrinkled like a crumpled paper bag. He wore a thick red knit sweater despite the heat inside, and his eyes narrowed the second Jalen stepped through the door.

"Haven't seen you since you were fifteen." Marcus proceeded to punch a few keys on his register. "You look sick. Don't matter that you lost weight. You still look sick. Are you?"

Jalen laughed lightly and then stopped abruptly. "Good to see you too, Marcus."

He waved him off, leaning forward on the counter. "Get outta my store," he snapped. "I ain't got no M&M's and pickles for you."

Tink and Everett walked in behind Jalen, their shoulders brushing against the doorframe. As Jalen did everything but leave, Tink flicked a lighter open and closed, the small flame dancing briefly before disappearing again. Everett stayed quiet, his hands shoved into his coat pockets, his eyes scanning the store.

"I ain't here to cause trouble," he said, though his tone made it sound like a lie.

The old man didn't budge. "I said get out."

Jalen stopped a few feet from the counter. "You and me both know I'm not doing that. Don't we?"

Marcus sighed.

"You gonna tell me everything you know about Lockland," he said, his voice low and demanding.

"I ain't tellin' you nothin'. Say what you want, Lockland is a good man. And you don't get to fuck with him, not around here."

Tink smirked, leaning against one of the shelves. "Pops, don't make this harder than it has to be."

"You can't scare me. I been here longer than you been alive."

Jalen pressed. "He was living with you, but I never knew why. So who is his family? Where did that nigga come from?"

Tink and Everett frowned. "Wait...Jalen not your real brother?"

"Nah."

"Why you ain't tell us?" Everett asked.

The truth was it was embarrassing. For his mother to choose a stray over her own child hurt. So he didn't want anyone knowing, especially not his friends who looked up to him. And who he needed. At the same time Lockland appeared to come from nowhere and he wanted more details.

Jalen ignored his friends and leaned in closer to the counter, his voice dropping to a near whisper. "Tell me what you know...or else."

FLASHBACK

The old apartment building in east Baltimore seemed to complain with every gust of wind.

Cracks ran up the walls like veins, and the sound of stolen electricity buzzed through makeshift wires that snaked along the floorboards, feeding off nearby streetlights. Extension cords ran through broken windows and tied into nearby stores, their connections barely holding together with duct tape and frayed ends. Lights flickered constantly, but in ten-year-old Lockland's home, it beat living in the dark.

Lockland sat on the thin mattress in the corner of the room, his knees pulled to his chest. He was shivering, his breath visible in the freezing air. His toes were numb inside his too-small socks, the holes letting the cold seep in.

"I'm freezing, mama," he whispered.

"Hush, boy. You always cold!" Tracey, snapped, slamming her hand against the wall. Her voice echoed through the apartment, startling him. She paced back and forth, her thin frame wrapped in a cheap faux-fur coat that smelled of stale perfume. Her face was tight, her movements jittery like she couldn't sit still.

Her ass was cold too, for sure.

Lisa, his 22-year-old sister, sat cross-legged on a folding chair, puffing on a cigarette. "You gotta chill, Lock," she said, blowing the smoke out in a slow stream. "We all cold so ain't no sense in stating the obvious."

Lockland hugged himself tighter, tears pooling in his eyes. He tried not to cry, but his chest ached from holding it in so long. Why couldn't she be a better mother? Why couldn't she love him and make him feel safe?

It was exhausting not having a woman to care for him, especially since his father had died many years earlier in a car accident. He prayed for something, anything to change, but all of his prayers had gone unanswered.

"Exactly...you think you the only one sufferin'?" Tracey hollered, spinning around to face him. "You think this easy for us? Huh? We all doin' what we gotta do to get by!"

Lockland flinched, his small body curling tighter into itself.

Tracey shook her head, muttering under her breath. "When we make a come-up, we outta here. You hear me? We gonna move somewhere nice. You just gotta wait."

It was a lie. Lockland knew it, even at ten-years-old. She always said the same thing, and nothing ever changed.

Lisa stubbed out her cigarette on the windowsill, the ashes falling into a chipped cup. "Mama, let's go. We got people waitin'."

"Fucking with his ass I almost forgot," Tracey sighed, grabbing her purse from the broken table by the door. "Stay put," she told Lockland, pointing a long, painted nail at him. "And don't touch nothin'. We'll be back later."

Lockland didn't answer. He just stared at the floor as they left, the sound of their heels clicking down the hallway until it faded in the distance.

The apartment was silent, except for the low dialogue coming from the small TV. Lockland sat watching *Life,* the old movie with Eddie Murphy and Martin Lawrence. It was his favorite, and every time Lisa Nicole Carson appeared on the screen, he couldn't help but stare.

She was stunning, and there was something about the way she asked Martin why he wanted to go home. In Lockland's young mind, it felt like maybe she wanted him to stay with her instead.

And if it were him? He knew he would.

When his stomach growled, he ignored it, but his fingers were stiff from the cold, and his body ached from shivering so much.

Needing to feel warmth, his eyes landed on his mother's lighter, sitting on the windowsill next to a pile of old newspapers. She used it frequently to chain smoke and so its metallic surface was scratched and worn.

He had an idea!

Lockland reached for it, his small hand trembling as he picked it up. He flicked the wheel, and the tiny flame danced to life in the dark room.

It was warm and hypnotizing.

Wanting to make it bigger, and cozier, he grabbed a piece of newspaper and held it over the flame. The edges curled and blackened before catching fire, the warmth spreading up the paper. Lockland smiled lightly, holding it close to his chest for a moment before setting it on the floor.

And then it happened.

The fire spread faster than he expected.

The flames licked at the edge of the mattress, then climbed higher, eating away at the peeling wallpaper. Smoke filled the room, thick and choking, burning his throat and eyes. Lockland coughed, stumbling back as the heat grew unbearable.

What could he do?

Nothing.

So he ran.

The hallway was chaos, neighbors shouting and pushing past each other, their faces wild with fear. The smell of burning wood and plastic filled the air. Lockland didn't stop as the freezing night air hit him like a slap.

He was still cold, but suddenly he didn't care.

The corner store was quiet when Lockland stumbled in, his clothes singed, and his face streaked with soot. A younger Marcus who sat behind the counter looked up and frowned when he saw the child.

"What the hell happened to you, boy?" He asked, his voice rough.

Lockland didn't answer.

He just stood there, trembling, his teeth chattering. He knew his mother wasn't about shit. And his sister was next in line to be about nothing too, so his heart warmed for him.

Marcus sighed, motioning for him to come closer. "Alright, sit down. Don't say nothin' yet. Let me get you somethin' to drink and a wet nap to wipe your face. Then tell me only what you want me to know."

A few days later, Lockland was sweeping the floor of the store when the bell above the door jingled. He looked up and froze.

Inside walked the prettiest woman he'd seen in a long time.

It was Lisa Nicole Carson...or actually Cakes.

She was wearing a pink dress, and her large breasts bounced lightly as she moved through the aisles. The men who were inside picking a few things, paused to give her their undivided, because she was that bad. Her hair draped down the sides of her face and she tucked it behind her ear as she continued her stroll.

Lockland stared at her, something warm stirring in his chest.

"Excuse me, young man," she said, her voice kind but firm. "Could you help me find the flour?"

He jumped at first. He wasn't even sure she saw him.

But of course he could help.

Lockland nodded quickly, grabbing the bag off the shelf and following her to the counter. He watched as she handed the old man a few bills, then struggled to carry the heavy bag back to her car. But he would be damned if he allowed her to do it on her own.

"I'll take it for you."

She was impressed. "I got it you know."

"It really is fine," Lockland insisted. "I got it. Trust me."

Cakes smiled, the kind of smile that felt genuine, and let him take the bag. "Well, aren't you sweet," she said as he loaded it into her trunk.

"Wish I could say the same about my own damn son."

That's when he saw him.

Inside the car, a boy about Lockland's age sat slouched in the back seat.

It was Jalen.

He didn't even bother to look his way.

It took Lockland a minute but eventually he found out where Jalen and Cakes lived. All he had to do was give free food to Turner, the neighborhood dopehead, which he sold, and he would sing like a bird.

He may have been young, but the boy had a plan.

He wanted Lisa Nicole Carson, he meant, Cakes to be his mother. So he had to get to work.

Walking up to their second-floor apartment building, Lockland started bringing Jalen snacks from the corner store...chips, candy bars, whatever he could grab. At first, Jalen was suspicious, but soon he started to warm up, letting

Lockland hang around more often. Before long, a few months, the two were inseparable.

And although Jalen's weight grew more intense, he didn't seem to mind because he was too young to comprehend the future damage to his body. Now it was time for Lockland to push further.

He wanted in the house.

"You should ask your mom if I can stay over sometime," Lockland said one day, his voice casual but hopeful.

Jalen shrugged. "You wanna live with me?"

"Yeah...I mean Mr. Marcus is nice but I don't have no place to sleep that's my own. Too many boxes and mice."

"I'll ask her...but you won't like it if she says yes."

"Why?"

"She's too mean."

Lies. He loved the woman already, so he knew Jalen was off.

A week later, Cakes invited Lockland to dinner. "You're always so polite," she said with a smile. "And such a hard worker. You're welcome anytime."

Before long Jalen saw something else happening.

Lockland was the kid he never was to his mother. He helped her in ways that Jalen found boring and now it was causing a wedge between them that he claimed he didn't care about.

With time, he moved in and took over.

Lockland wasn't just a foster child.

He became her favorite child.

And things would never be the same.

CHAPTER SIX

Shannon paced toward her front door, the hardwood floors creaked beneath her feet as she approached. When she opened the door she saw the Dust Boys standing there, their presence as familiar as it was foreboding.

Taking a deep breath, she pushed the door open wider. "He's in the back," she crossed her arms over her chest. "I'll make coffee."

The three men nodded, stepping inside, their heavy boots scuffing the worn floor. Without another word, they made their way to her bedroom. The room was hazy, the scent of lavender from a neglected candle lingering in the air. Lockland was propped on the edge of the bed, his back in their direction as he stared out the rain-speckled window.

"Y'all strapped?"

"I forgot my gun in the house," Dion said.

"We got ours," Wakes said, shaking his head at Dion.

"Any word on Jalen?" Lockland asked, his voice low and steady.

The Dust Boys exchanged uneasy glances.

"Hey, man, I'm really sorry about Cakes. I know you—."

"I don't wanna hear it. The only thing I wanna hear is that nigga's location. That's it."

"We been looking," Wakes continued, his voice trailing off.

"So you got nothing," Lockland interrupted, his tone angry.

The men looked at each other again. Finally, Dion stepped forward. "We put the money out there, just like you told us, but for now, it's a ghost town."

Lockland sighed deeply, his shoulders slumping slightly. "Go. I'll hit back later."

The Dust Boys nodded and turned to leave, their movements quiet and subdued. On their way out, they hugged Shannon briefly before disappearing through the door.

Now alone, she lingered near the kitchen, her hands gripping the counter as she stared down at the scuffed surface. She shook her head just as she heard Lockland's heavy footsteps approaching and she turned to face him.

"I'm sorry, but I can't do this with you," she said softly, her voice barely above a whisper.

Lockland nodded. "I know. And I'm not asking you to, baby."

"Don't call me that. Not anymore." She took a deep breath, her eyes meeting his. "I know it seems like forever…a year, but—"

"You don't have to explain," he said, cutting her off gently. "Losing our daughter…and the way it was done…will always be raw. I just want you to know I'm here. It's just that today, I didn't have anywhere else to turn." Lockland stepped closer, pressing a gentle kiss to her cheek before heading to the door.

"Lock, find him. I need you to finish this."

Lockland paused, nodded without turning back, and walked toward his Impala. The rain had eased into a soft drizzle, the cool air brushing against his face as he climbed into the car.

When he arrived home, the smell of damp wood and disarray greeted him. Carl sat on the porch, his unseeing eyes seemingly fixed on the distance.

"Your aunt's here," he said simply.

"Saw the car." Lockland nodded.

"And I'm sorry that I wasn't here when they took everything. I would've—"

"You don't gotta say all that," Lockland interrupted, his voice soft but firm. "I already know where you stood with my mother."

"Jalen is troubled," he continued. "I mean, he really needs help."

"I would've given him that awhile back. But now when I catch the nigga he's dead."

"Respect." Carl dipped his head in acknowledgment, his hands resting on his knees. When soft talk was done, Lockland opened the door and stepped inside.

Myra was sweeping the living room, her movements brisk but deliberate. She put the entire place back together, but he wanted to be alone. The door creaked slightly behind him, and Lockland left it open, knowing he wanted her to leave quickly. Not because he didn't love her, he did, but now wasn't the time.

"I know what you're about to do," Myra said, not bothering to look up from her task. "I just want you to remain clear on your focus. And clear on your promise to your mother. I could be wrong but I'm sure she don't want you to kill her child."

Cap.

She gave him her blessing.

Lockland leaned against the wall, crossing his arms as he listened.

"So why you here?"

"To stop you from snapping. Burying yourself and what Cakes gave up to love you."

He pushed the door open wider. Then he walked over and kissed her on the forehead. "Get out. I'll be in touch later."

She nodded and left him alone. A few minutes after she left Carl started yelling, "Whoa, man! Whoa, man!"

Lockland's head snapped toward the door, his eyes narrowing.

"Whoa, man!" Carl called again, louder this time.

When he saw who set him off, Lockland bolted out the door, his boots pounding against the wooden steps. He jumped the fence and sprinted toward his Impala. The car roared to life as he peeled out of the driveway, his tires screeching against the wet pavement.

Grace walked out of the gas station, the scent of burnt coffee and motor oil lingering in the air. She had just paid for her gas and was halfway to her car when she realized she'd forgotten to grab mint gum. With a sigh, she turned back, her boots clicking softly on the pavement. Retracing her steps, she reentered and made her purchase.

When she stepped back outside, the cool evening air brushing against her skin, she froze. There, standing by her car, was Lockland. His tall frame was angled just right, and even in the bright glow of the station's fluorescent lights, his presence was magnetic. He was pumping her gas, his movements smooth and deliberate.

Grace took a deep breath and glided toward him. Her heart thumped in her chest, but he didn't know. However, what she did peep immediately was the silhouette of the gun under his shirt in front of his pants.

"I could've done that myself," she said in an amused but irritated tone.

"I figured you wanted me to," Lockland replied plainly, his eyes fixed on the pump as he squeezed the handle, ensuring every drop of gas she'd paid for made it into the tank. When the pump clicked, signaling the tank was full, he released the handle and turned to her. "Since you been popping up at my mother's house and following me around for the last few days."

Grace blinked several times, a nervous habit she wished she could be rid of. "So you've been seeing me all this time?"

Silence.

"There are some things that—" she began, but he cut her off.

"You police," he stated bluntly, his eyes narrowing slightly. On her passenger seat there was a gold badge inside of her brown purse. He nodded toward it.

"Perceptive."

Lockland remained serious. "Listen, I got shit going on right now. And I know you wouldn't be following me if you didn't have questions. So before you do anything, just give me five minutes of your time."

CHAPTER SEVEN

Memory climbed the stairs to her boyfriend's apartment, her stomach churning with each step. The stench was unbearable...stale urine, the sour tang of unwashed bodies, and the pungent spices seeping from neighboring kitchens. The odor was so toxic she had to swallow hard to keep herself from gagging.

The only thing that brought a small smile to her face was Davis. His hand gripped hers firmly as they ascended the stairwell, a bag of her unwashed clothes hanging heavy in her other hand. His pride was evident, for the first time ever, he was bringing her to his apartment, a place she didn't even know he occupied.

The thought of them having somewhere private to be together, a space to call their own, filled her with giddy anticipation. So what if it's a mess. She thought. I can clean it up and make the shit liveable.

"You good?" Davis asked, glancing at her with a confident grin.

Memory nodded.

"I'm so glad you finally said yes to moving in with me. It's not the best, but I know we can make it work."

She nodded again, her heart swelling. When it came to recognizing game, she was on a grade school level, and he loved it too.

That way he could take full advantage.

Once at the door, Davis pulled his keys from his pocket and unlocked it before shoving once to enter. The moment the door creaked open, the reality hit her like a beef burp to the face.

The apartment was far worse than she had imagined. Trash was scattered across the floor in such quantities that she couldn't see the carpet beneath it. The smell was overpowering with rotting food and a stale air that had likely gone uncirculated for weeks. Memory covered her nose as she kicked a few garbage bags aside, making a narrow path into the room. She placed her own trash bag gently against the wall by the door, terrified it might get lost in the chaos.

I can't live here, she thought.

The moment she was prepared to let him know, Davis walked up behind her. His hands slid around her waist as he turned her toward him.

And before she could argue, he kissed her softly. "You good?"

"I...I think so."

"Listen, don't be worried about all this shit. Once you clean it up, we're gonna be good here."

"Me?"

"You my girl right?"

Memory hesitated, her unease finally bubbling to the surface. "I don't know about this." For the first time, she let her concern show. Until now, she'd let Davis believe she would go along with anything he wanted, but this...this was too much.

"Trust me," he said, flashing her a smile. "This is gonna work out. Besides, once you get that money from your mom's life insurance policy, we can get someplace better. Together."

His words stung, but his kiss, quick and sweet, softened the blow. She wanted to believe that the future he planned for her was gonna be right, but this was a bad start.

"I can't wait for everybody to know that me and my girl are finally doing the right thing by each other. But listen..." He stepped back. "I gotta go get us something to eat. You got any spare change on you?"

Memory frowned and dragged a hand down her face. "Oh, um, let me see," she walked to her bag near the door. Next she knelt down and rummaged through it a moment. When she felt her knee slip and slide she saw it was a squished banana peel pressed against her kneecap.

It took everything real for her not to scream.

Digging deeper into her bag, she finally found her pink wallet. She opened it, pulling out one of the two twenties tucked inside and handed it to him. "Here you go."

He glared. "What are we, ten years old? Give me the other one too," he said casually, as if he wasn't begging. "We grown ass people 'round here."

Memory hesitated and peeled the second bill from the wallet and placed it in his hand. Davis grinned, kissed her forehead, and said, "I'll be back. Like I said, clean this bitch up. Good too."

The door slammed and Memory sank downward. The weight of everything...her mother's death, the filthy apartment and Davis' uneasy demands burned her hard. She wanted to run, but she had a feeling there was nowhere to go. She was stuck.

And then she remembered her mother's words she would repeat constantly. "Sooner or later everyone pays what they owe."

CHAPTER EIGHT

Lockland sat inside a small diner, the kind with a bar that was usually occupied with loud mouthed regulars feeling good off their bartender's extra pours. The air was thick with the aroma of fried chicken and spices while the overhead lighting cast a soft glow, making his silver chain sparkle.

"How long did you know I was looking for you?" She asked, her tone carrying a hint of challenge.

Lockland leaned back slightly, a sly smile on his face. "I see you all the time. So whenever I hear Carl yell out, 'Whoa, man,' I know he's talking to me."

"What does that mean?"

"Woman...he smells the perfume you wear and didn't want to let you know he was on to you."

She shook her head. "I'm slipping. I was wondering what that was about," she added. "I knew he was blind but that's why I didn't mind him knowing I was there."

"Just because you're blind don't mean you aren't aware."

"I learn something new every day."

Lockland leaned forward slightly, his tone shifting to something quieter, almost vulnerable. He felt in his heart this was about the apartment fire that he had been running from for most of his life. Besides, ten people died and they never got down to the bottom of the who and why.

"Listen, I don't know what case you got on me, but I need you to fall the fuck back right now."

"And why would I do that?"

"My mother just died, and I intend on getting out the game behind that."

"So you want me to let you do more crime?" She asked, her voice laced with sarcasm just as the waitress arrived, placing steaming platters of fried chicken and fries in front of them.

"What if I don't do what you're asking, Lockland?"

"Just give me a week and a half. And after that anything you want to know, I'll tell you."

She raised an eyebrow, leaning back slightly in her chair. Even now he held the handle of the gun through the fabric of his shirt. "You always carry a gun on you? Are you licensed to carry?"

Silence.

"Will you fall back?" He said sterner.

"So what am I supposed to tell the bosses between now and then?"

Lockland's smile disappeared. "I don't want to hurt you. I really don't. I just need you to back off. That's it."

She studied him for a bit longer. Finally she looked at the food. "You said this chicken good, huh?"

"The best."

The night air was crisp, carrying the distant smell of fried food and car exhaust as Grace stepped out of the restaurant. Lockland walked beside her.

Lockland nodded, his dark eyes scanning the block. "Stay safe out here," he said, his voice low and even, before turning and walking in the opposite direction.

Grace's smile lingered for a moment, then dropped as soon as he turned the corner. She adjusted her jacket, tucking her hands into her pockets as she approached the group.

Jalen leaned against the light pole, his arms crossed, his face twisted into a sinister grin. Tink stood to his left, his lighter flicking open and closed, the tiny flame dancing with each snap. Everett was on the other side, his hands shoved deep into his coat pockets, his eyes scanning the street lazily.

"What we got?" Jalen said, his grin widening as Grace stopped in front of them.

Grace laughed. "You won't believe this shit...he thinks I'm *police*. 'Cause of my investigation badge."

Jalen's eyebrows shot up, his grin turning to a laugh. "I know you lyin'. Ain't no way it's that easy."

"Dead ass serious," Grace replied, leaning in slightly. "Man's paranoid as fuck."

Jalen shook his head, letting out a low chuckle. "You mean I hid from this nigga for a whole year just for him to basically kill himself?" His voice dropped slightly, his tone darker. "Still holdin' onto that guilt, huh? Over that fire."

Grace tilted her head. "Fire?"

"Let's just say I learned a little somethin' when I paid Marcus a visit with Tink and Everett. Since he think you police, that will be the angle. We will make it about the fire. And when you get a chance, put one in his head."

Grace leaned back, crossing her arms over her chest. "One problem, though," she said, her voice turning serious. "He always has his hand on his weapon. I've seen it. He doesn't even let it go when he's eating."

"I know that...fuck you think I hired you for?" He paused. "It's easier for a female to get at him. Fuck him if you got to. Just remember to show me his blood when it's all said and done. And I'ma start fucking with him hard in the background. Because there is one thing people don't know about him...that nigga is crazy."

CHAPTER NINE

The night air was heavy, the kind that clung to the skin and made every breath feel just a little too thick. Crickets chirped relentlessly in the overgrown grass that brushed against their legs, the blades tugging at their jeans as they hung in place.

Lockland stood in front of the Dust Boys, his gaze steady and unyielding. "Okay, I laid out a plan. A plan we have to execute in seven days. That's the amount of days I got to bury, ma."

Wakes, always the strategist, shifted his weight slightly and exchanged a glance with the others. Usually reserved, he had an air of calmness. Once a chess prodigy, Wakes had fallen into crime after losing his scholarship, a twist of fate that landed him with the Dust Boys.

"We been trying to find this nigga for over a year," Wakes reminded him, his tone measured. "And now you think we gonna be able to find him in seven days?"

"Exactly," Dion added. Dion was the enforcer who carried out the group's plans with no questions asked. Hot-headed and impulsive, Dion was always ready for a fight, but his devotion grounded him.

For the moment.

"I'm with you, Lockland," Dion continued, fists clenched. "I'll burn the whole city looking for that nigga. I just want to make sure that when we do this, it's gonna get you what you want."

Lockland shook his head, his chain glinting faintly in the dim light. "Man, I wouldn't be talking to y'all if I didn't think this is what I wanted."

"I hear you," Dion replied, nodding. "I just need us to apply more pressure than we ever have. Brother or not."

Shoes, the wild card of the group, crossed his arms and leaned against the crumbling fence. Nicknamed for his obsession with footwear, he was unpredictable and could turn any situation into chaos if convinced enough.

"There's one thing I don't get," Shoes said, his voice tinged with skepticism. "Why we going so hard right now? If it was war, we could've done this earlier."

"I know why we couldn't go hard before," Wakes said quietly, his gaze steady as he nodded toward Lockland. "Cakes was alive. Wasn't trying to kill her son no matter how much she loved the nigga."

Lockland exhaled deeply, the weight of Wakes' words settling over the group. For a moment, the crickets seemed louder, the night darker.

"With my mother gone," Lockland said, his voice low but charged with intensity, "there's nothing that's gonna stop me from laying hands on this nigga. I know he's out there smiling, thinking shit sweet. He'll find out soon enough though. Because what he did...what he did...twisted me in ways I can't rest from."

The Dust Boys stood silently, the gravity of his words pressing down on them. Something happened between him, Jalen and his daughter Asia that he never revealed. Still, they could tell he was different. Not only that, but he had also been smoking weed, something that normally caused him extreme paranoia.

"My only question to y'all is, are you with me or not?"

Wakes straightened, his face serious as he nodded. "To the casket."

"To the casket," Dion echoed.

Shoes grinned. "You already know."

Suddenly Lockland's phone buzzed for the fifteenth time with the funeral home's number glaring on the screen. He knew he wanted a date for services, but he couldn't give him one because Jalen was still breathing.

Cakes was clear, don't bury her until he finished his beefs.

"You gotta see what they want," Wakes said.

Lockland answered. "I already know you want me to lock in a date. I'll hit you when –."

"It's not about that!" The funeral director's voice on the other end was strained, trembling slightly. "I need you to come here and I need you to come now."

Lockland exchanged a glance with Dion. "Give me fifteen."

True to his word, Lockland stood in the funeral home, the scent of flowers and antiseptic clinging to the air. The low lighting made the room feel smaller and the atmosphere thick with unease. The Dust Boys flanked his side, their presence as silent and heavy as a storm cloud.

"So you telling me you didn't protect my mother's casket?"

"I'm sorry..."

"Don't be sorry, nigga," Wakes said. "Take us to her."

The funeral director led them to the back, his nervousness palpable in the way he wrung his hands and avoided eye contact. Lockland's eyes narrowed as he approached the casket. The moment he saw it, his breath caught in his chest.

The underlid of the casket was defaced, white paint scrawled across it in jagged letters: YOU CAN'T FIND A GHOST.

Lockland's blood boiled. His fists clenched at his sides as he felt a surge of rage bubbling up, threatening to spill over. He spun on his heel, his voice like a whip. "Who did this?"

The funeral director stuttered. "W...we don't know."

Removing his gun from his waist, he placed it in his face. "Fuck you mean you don't know?" Lockland roared, his voice echoing off the sterile walls. "I left her in your possession. You better tell me something, nigga."

"I said I don't—."

Lockland shot past his ear, causing the man to hold both sides of his face. "The next one going in your mouth."

"He a square, man," Wakes reminded him. "Not right here."

Saved by a killer, Lockland tucked his gun and Dion stepped forward and grabbed the director by the lapels of his suit. The man was hoisted slightly off the ground, his feet barely scraping earth.

"Open your mouth or die quick, bitch," Dion growled, his voice low and menacing.

"He must wanna be in a casket right next to her," Shoes laughed.

The director raised his hands in surrender, his voice trembling as he gasped, "Honestly, I don't know what happened. All I know is that the cameras showed someone pulling up toward the back. After that, the cameras went black."

"What did they look like?" Dion demanded, his grip tightening. "You gotta tell us something."

"He had a stumble like walk. Like he would fall over. Like he was high or something."

The director's description was halting but vivid enough for Lockland's mind to conjure a chilling image. The details were disturbingly familiar, striking too close to home. His stomach twisted, a thought forming like a dark shadow in his mind.

Could Turner have reached that low?

Lockland forced the thought away for the moment. "Pick out another casket."

Dion let the man drop unceremoniously to the ground, and the director scrambled to straighten himself, his breath coming in shallow gasps.

"And the fee is on you," Lockland added, his tone final.

"Of course, sir. Of course. It won't happen again," the director said, his voice trembling. They were walking toward the door when he said, "But, sir?"

All four turned toward him.

"When will you bury her? It's been one day since she's been embalmed. Technically we should bury her and have the funeral in 6 more days."

"Just pick another casket."

Without another word, the four of them left, their footsteps heavy and purposeful as they exited into the cool night air. The Dust Boys piled into the truck.

"Where we rolling now?" Dion asked, breaking the silence.

Lockland's knuckles tightened around the steering wheel. "To find Turner's bitch ass."

Cell phone in hand, Turner lay sprawled on his dingy bed, the smell of mildew clinging to the sheets. The air in the room was thick, suffocating.

Suddenly, a sharp pain gripped his stomach, forcing a groan from his lips. The pain intensified, twisting like a blade, and before he knew it, the excruciating need to go to the bathroom overtook him.

He stumbled out of bed, clutching his belly, his movements frantic and jerky. His cell phone locked in his grip. The wooden floorboards grumbled under his weight as he hurried to the door. But when he reached it, he stopped short. Wakes was there, standing tall and immovable, blocking his path. Turner's breath hitched as panic set in.

"What the hell is this?" He demanded, his voice trembling as much from the pain as from the fear creeping into his chest.

He wasn't alone.

Turner spun rapidly, and his gaze landed on Dion. The big man stood in the corner, cracking his knuckles while Shoes, leaned casually against the wall, his face calm but his eyes focused, like a predator waiting for the right moment to strike.

But it wasn't until Turner turned to his right that the true weight of his situation hit him.

Lockland stood there, his presence dominating the room. His expression was cold, his eyes dark and unrelenting. Turner's legs weakened, and he staggered slightly.

"What's going on?" Turner gasped.

"So you that much of a *do anything for money ass nigga*?" Lockland took a step closer, eying the phone. "You really would go as low as to desecrate our mother's casket?"

"I don't know what you—"

Dion stole him in the jaw, forcing him silent.

"I don't believe you," Lockland replied, his tone deadly calm. "So I don't even want you finishing the rest."

Turner shifted uncomfortably, the pain in his stomach intensifying and matching the one in his bleeding mouth. "Just...just get out my way," he said, his voice rising in desperation. "I need to shit!"

But Lockland didn't move.

None of them did.

Instead, he stepped closer, his voice dropping to a dangerous whisper. "I want you to hear me, and I want you to hear me good," he said, his eyes boring into Turner's. "For the rest of your life, you gonna have to worry about what you put in your mouth. You gonna have to wonder if I've swapped out whatever pill you sucking back for something... like I just gave you tonight. And because you a dopehead you won't be able to do shit about it, even though it might kill you."

Turner's eyes widened in horror. "What you do?" He felt faint. "When...how?"

"Don't worry about all that. You don't know what I'm capable of and I'm warning you to stay out the way."

Turner staggered back, his legs barely holding him up as fear and pain overwhelmed him. Lockland took one last, icy glance at him before heading for the door. His footsteps echoed ominously in the silent room.

"Where you going?"

"I know where Jalen at so I'm about to kill that nigga," he lied.

"Uh...why you telling me though?" Turner pretended like he didn't care but his expression told him different. "I haven't seen him in years."

"I hear you talking."

Shoes stepped out the house, his sneakers crunching against the gravel driveway as he made his way to the truck. His face was twisted in annoyance, his hands shoved deep into his pockets as he approached the truck where Lockland, Wakes, and Dion sat waiting.

He climbed into the passenger seat, slamming the door harder than necessary. "Thanks a lot for leaving me in that bitch," he said, his voice dripping with sarcasm. "The nigga shit his pants."

Dion let out a loud laugh from the backseat, his voice booming. "You serious? Why he do that?"

Shoes shot him a glare. "Because I wouldn't let him go. Tried to get at his phone but he had it with him the whole time. You should've just let me take it," he said to Lockland.

"Nah, that ain't the plan." His eyes remained locked on Turner's house. "The plan was to scare him to do what I need next."

Fifteen minutes later, the front door flew open, and Turner stumbled out. He clutched his stomach as he half-ran, half-hobbled toward the sidewalk, his stained pants still clinging to him.

Lockland smiled.

"Ain't no fucking way," Wakes said, sitting upright. "He still wearing them shitty ass pants!"

Lockland didn't react.

His gaze followed Turner, unyielding. He watched as his brother disappeared down the street, his movements frantic and erratic, like a man running from more than just embarrassment.

"Just like I thought, he's going to Jalen," Lockland said finally, his voice low and angry.

The weight of his words settled over the truck like a heavy fog. No one questioned him. They all knew better than to doubt Lockland when he spoke with such certainty.

"Follow him?" Wakes asked after a moment.

Lockland nodded once. Without another word, they crept from behind.

From the darkness, Lockland and the Dust Boys followed Turner, who drove haphazardly down the dimly lit road.

Turner finally parked near an ambulance, its worn exterior illuminated by the weak overhead light of the parking lot. The sight was strange, out of place, and immediately raised suspicion.

"What he about to do?" Wakes asked.

“Whatever it is, won’t be good,” Dion replied, his tone edged with impatience. His broad shoulders were tense, his hand resting on the grip of his pistol.

“I say we yank him,” Dion added.

Shoes let out a low chuckle, shaking his head. “Didn’t I just tell y’all? He’s still wearing the same pants. Let’s at least give the man a chance to see what he up to first before we put his funky ass in here.”

They all stayed focused on Turner’s ride, their eyes locked. Lockland, however, caught something in the rearview mirror that fucked his head up.

His jaw tightened.

“I can’t believe this shit,” he said under his breath.

“What is it?” The others asked almost in unison, their hands already moving toward their hammers.

“Listen,” Lockland said, his voice calm but firm. “Y’all keep watching my brother. Don’t let him out your sight.”

Wakes frowned. “Should one of us go with you?”

“Nah, it’s the cop,” Lockland replied.

Before anyone could dispute, he slipped out of the truck and ran toward the back to a sleek black Mercedes parked far behind, but not far enough to escape his gaze. He opened the passenger door and slid in smoothly. The woman in the driver's seat barely glanced at him as they pulled away, their car disappearing into the night.

Back in the truck, Wakes, Dion, and Shoes continued to watch Turner's car and the ambulance. Minutes passed, each one stretching into eternity as Turner remained inside, unmoving.

"Y'all see that?" Wakes asked, his eyes narrowing as he peered into the darkness.

"See what?" Dion replied, his body tensing as his hand tightened around his weapon.

Wakes shook his head. "I think...I think he walked us into a trap."

Before anyone could react, the night erupted with chaos. Bullets rained down on their vehicle, the sharp cracks of gunfire splitting the air and the car. The first bullets shattered the windshield, sending shards of glass cascading onto their laps. The metallic tang of gunpowder filled their noses as the barrage continued.

Wakes, always quick to react, lowered his body and slammed the truck into reverse. The tires screeched against the asphalt, the vehicle jerking backward as he hunched lower in his seat. Dion and Shoes followed suit, ducking down to avoid the hail of bullets that ripped through the cabin. The sound of the gunfire was deafening.

They couldn't fire back; they had no clear sight of their attackers. Shadows moved in the periphery, but the attackers stayed hidden, their positions concealed.

"Hold on!" Wakes yelled as he maneuvered the truck, his knuckles white against the wheel.

The Dust Boys' hearts pounded as Wakes managed to steer them away from the scene, the truck swerving wildly as they made their escape. With God's grace, and maybe even Cakes' spirit, the gunfire faded behind them.

Lockland sat in the passenger seat as Grace drove aimlessly through the city streets. She glanced over at him, and noticed his hand still hovered over his trigger. The hum of the engine filled the silence.

Finally he turned his head in her direction. "Fuck is wrong with you?"

She looked at his chiseled chest and then his eyes. "I don't know what—."

"I get you feel you gotta watch me. But sneaking in the background not gonna work. Do you want me to kill your ass?"

"Threatening an officer?"

"Yes."

Grace glanced at him, her expression unbothered. "I didn't know you were up to something."

"Who said I was up to something?"

"I can tell. Besides, I'm just protecting my investment."

"So, now I'm your investment?" Lockland repeated, raising an eyebrow.

"It was your idea to have me hold off on my investigation, remember? That means you're going to have to give me something."

"Give you something like what?" He asked, his tone guarded.

"Your time. A little more information about who you are," she replied smoothly. "So I can appease the bosses."

Lockland smirked. "I thought you already knew everything about me."

She shook her head, her stare fixed on the road ahead. "If I knew everything, you'd be in jail right?"

The smirk deepened because for what he did he couldn't be arrested. He was a child. "So you can't arrest me because you don't have enough," he said, his voice dripping with amusement. Suddenly it felt like he had the upper hand. "What would make me wanna help you with that?"

Grace smiled, a glint of mischief in her eyes. "I know about the fire. Where many people died."

That would do it.

"And if you push me away, maybe I'll snatch little Memory up or even Shannon."

Now the gun was in full display, and he held it in his hand. "Don't fuck with me or my people."

"And you don't fuck with me either," She responded. Realizing the air was thick she decided to lighten the mood. "What happened with Shannon?"

"My little girl...our little girl was killed."

"How?" She seriously didn't know.

"I don't wanna get into that right now."

She nodded and sighed. "Okay, to prove you can trust me...how about I tell you something about myself?"

"I like where this direction is going better. So what you want me to know?"

She chuckled softly. "I've gone back to that chicken spot three times since I last saw you."

Lockland grinned. "Ain't that cute."

Although she attempted to lighten the mood, there was something in her tone, something steady and sure, that made Lockland uneasy. But before he could dwell on it, his phone buzzed in his pocket. He answered it without excusing himself, his eyes narrowing as he listened.

"You okay?" He asked, his voice softening slightly. A pause, then, "I'm on my way."

When he hung up, Grace was watching him, curiosity evident on her face. "Is everything good?"

Lockland nodded. "I need you to drop me off somewhere. Don't ask questions."

She raised an eyebrow but didn't press. Following his directions...right here, left there, another right...they eventually pulled up in front of Shannon's house.

"I'll be in touch," Lockland said as he climbed out of the car. "But don't follow me again."

Grace gave him a short nod and pulled away, her taillights disappearing into the night. Lockland took a deep breath before stepping inside. The door was open, and he found Shannon sitting on the floor in the living room. Her hair was disheveled, her eyes red and puffy. She didn't even look up as he approached.

"What happened, baby?" He asked gently, crouching beside her. "You gonna make me spin out. You gotta tell me something!"

"Somebody...somebody called my house today and said...said that they are glad that my daughter is dead."

Lockland snapped.

It was Jalen and he was starting to see black. He just knew he was involved.

He breathed deeply. "What you need from me?"

"I just...I just need you to hold me," she whispered, her voice trembling.

Without a word, Lockland scooped her up and carried her to the bed. He lay down beside her, wrapping his arms around her as she buried her face in his chest. For a long time, they stayed as one, the silence filled only with her soft sobs.

Then she faced away from him and he figured something else was in play as her soft ass pressed against his dick.

So, he pushed down his boxers and slipped inside of her. She was wet...real wet and he loved it. Biting down softly on her shoulder he placed a warm hand on her hip and rocked back and forth sideways.

The longer he did it, the gushier she got and she moaned his name. "Lock...I still...I still..."

He wanted her to say it so badly.

Tell him she still loved him.

Tell him she forgave him, but the words never came. Instead she came on his dick moments before he did the same. Out of respect, he pulled out of her pussy and allowed the volcano to erupt in his hand. Kissing her back he wiped himself clean and their heavy breath crawled down together.

He was quick but it still hit.

And hour later his phone vibrated again. At first, he ignored it, unwilling to let go of Shannon even for a moment. But it kept buzzing, persistent and insistent. This time it was her who got annoyed.

Finally she spoke, her voice barely audible. "Just go. And lock the door on your way out."

"I'm sorry about this," he said, brushing a strand of hair from her face.

"You always are."

Lockland rolled out, jogging the three blocks to his own place. Sweat clung to his jacket by the time he arrived, but the sight that greeted him cooled him instantly. The Dust Boys stood by the bullet-riddled truck, their expressions looked as if they just saw a ghost.

"What happened?" Lockland demanded, his eyes scanning Wakes, Dion, and Shoes.

"We were ambushed, man," Wakes said, his voice tight. "Thing is, I don't even know where they were coming from. It was like they just emerged out of the darkness."

"Like ghosts," Lockland said as his gaze rolled between his friends. "Anybody get hit?"

"Nah, we good," Dion said, though the tension in his stance told a different story. "But listen, Lockland, we not letting you out of our sight anymore. Whatever that was, was about you not us. Something's about to go down. I don't know what, but it's coming."

Wakes nodded in agreement. "I already told my people they won't see me for a while. I'm in this."

Dion smirked faintly. "You know this like my house anyway. Ain't nothing for me to stay."

Lockland knew there was no use in him arguing. "After we lock in a plan, I gotta go snatch my sister. I don't care where she is, she coming with me."

"Let me make some calls," Wakes said. "I may be able to find something out."

Lockland sat in the dark kitchen, the clink of ice against his glass breaking the silence as he swirled his vodka. The chilled burn of the liquor was a brief distraction from the storm brewing inside him.

With one hand gripping the glass and the other holding his phone, he finally dialed Turner's number. It rang twice before his brother's voicemail came on.

"I know you had something to do with tonight. But we gonna catch your ass later. For now, I need to know where Memory is. Tell her to get at me. Or I'ma come find you."

CHAPTER TEN

Myra stirred her world-famous potato soup, the rich, savory aroma wafting through her kitchen. The thick broth bubbled gently on the stovetop, its surface glistening with love and the promise of a comforting meal. She turned the burner off with a practiced flick of her wrist and opened the oven, where the golden crust of sourdough bread greeted her with a garlicky, sweet warmth. The scent was intoxicating, and she inhaled deeply, savoring the moment.

Just as she reached for a knife to cut herself a slice and pour a bowl of soup, a knock at the door shattered her peaceful evening.

"Somebody always coming at the wrong damn time." She wiped her hands on the red apron tied snugly around her waist. Her irritation softened the moment she opened the door to see her nephew. She still fucked with him even though he through her out his house.

"Come on in," she said, her tone brightening with genuine warmth. "Hungry?"

Lockland nodded. "The boys are outside."

"Well, bring 'em in. You know I love Wakes and them."

"You always say Wakes and them. What about Dion and Shoes?"

"Let's not even play games," Myra said with a dramatic wave of her hand. "We all know Wakes in the line to hit this pussy."

"What the fuck?"

She laughed.

Lockland shook his head, stepping back onto the porch to call the Dust Boys. His voice rang out into the cool night air with a special call that they recognized immediately. Within seconds, they appeared, their silhouettes emerging from the shadows and into the warm glow of the porch light.

As they filed inside, Myra greeted each of them with hugs, but it was Wakes who planted a kiss on her cheek.

"I'll tell y'all one thing," Myra said with a grin. "Somebody raised y'all right, because y'all always smell good. Now go wash your hands."

Fifteen minutes later, the group sat around Myra's round kitchen table, bowls of steaming potato soup in front of them. The sourdough bread was already half gone, its crust crispy and the inside perfectly soft. The sound of spoons clinking against bowls mingled with occasional laughter as they enjoyed the meal.

When small talk was over, Lockland cleared his throat. It was time to get down to business.

"I need you to take care of Memory," he said, his voice steady but carrying a weight that silenced the room.

The Dust Boys glanced at each other, their gazes darting away. They knew how much Myra valued her peace and independence, and the thought of her taking on a rebellious teenager seemed unlikely.

"You know I got a crazy life," Myra said leaning back in her chair. "A busy one at that."

"I understand," Lockland replied, his tone calm but firm.

"And she don't listen."

"She won't have a choice."

Myra's eyes narrowed slightly as she studied her nephew. "Why you want me to do this, Lockland? Tell me straight up."

Lockland hesitated, then spoke. "Remember the woman I told you about earlier? Well I didn't get a chance to finish. She police. And she investigating me for something I did when I was a kid."

"If you were a kid you should be good."

"It's not getting locked up that I'm worried about. It's who may come looking for me once this story comes out."

She nodded. "How you know she a cop?"

"Saw the badge."

Myra shook her head, letting out a low sigh from hearing it all. Wakes reached over and squeezed her hand briefly, and she appreciated it more than she let on.

"I can't make no promises, nephew," she said finally, her voice steady but laced with emotion. "Because just like you, if I make a promise, I have to keep it. For now, I'll say give me some time. But if you need somebody to bust they gun, call me."

Lockland jolted awake, the room bathed in the soft light of early dawn. He sat on the edge of the bed, his feet pressing firmly against the cool wooden floor.

He called Memory a total of 62 times.

Nothing.

She was gonna make him snap.

Sure, she was technically grown, and sure, she didn't have to answer every call he made. But she was still his little sister. And if she thought she could move through this world without her big brother looking out for her...especially after the promise he made...she had another thing coming.

Reaching for the drawer, he pulled out a baggie. He knew it sometimes made him crazy, but he needed to be calm. So, using the blunt paper next to the sack, he rolled with the precision he was accustomed before turning the tip bright orange. Next he grabbed his gun and stuffed it on his right hip, the handle rubbing against his skin.

The blunt still between his lips, he walked into the living room, causing the creak of the floorboards to sound off. The Dust Boys were sprawled everywhere in varying states of sleep. Wakes was in the recliner, a gun resting precariously on his lap. Dion had claimed the couch, his gun balanced the same way. Shoes lay on the floor, his fingers curled tightly around the grip of his weapon, pointing it instinctively toward the front door.

The floorboards creaked again under Lockland's weight, and in a flash, all three were alert, their weapons raised and ready. For a brief, tense moment, silence blanketed the room.

"It's just me." Lockland said calmly, sending smoke signals through the air.

Recognizing him, they slowly lowered their guns, rubbing the sleep from their eyes. It was the weed between his lips that caused them great discomfort. After all, whenever he smoked, before long he dealt with psychosis and could be more dangerous than an unmanned insane asylum.

"You smoking a lot lately, huh?" Wakes asked carefully.

"Fuck it look like, nigga," he laughed lightly. "You want some?"

"I'll take it," Dion said, eager to get it from up under him.

After making the exchange he said, "Any word on Memory?"

"Nah, fam," Dion replied, shaking his head as he smoked from a blunt he wanted nothing to do with. His voice still carried the huskiness of sleep. "You want me to go knocking on doors?"

"Yeah, anybody know where Spare Change lays his head?" Wakes added.

Lockland sighed. “Nah. But I’m gonna find her. For now y’all niggas get up. We gotta go get my mama.”

They looked at one another in horror.

What did he just say?

He hadn’t found Jalen.

So he had two choices.

Break a promise or make a move.

He chose the move.

The night air was heavy as Lockland stood motionless, his tall frame silhouetted against the dim light. His presence was as much a part of these streets as the cracked asphalt beneath his boots.

Still shirtless, his tattooed neck peeked from the collar of his leather jacket, the ink snaking down his arms and continuing into his pants.

Slowly, deliberately, he approached the funeral home. It was mostly silent, except for the faint hum of distant traffic and the occasional bark of a stray dog. Once he was closer, he stopped by the side door, his shadow stretching across the fractured brick wall.

Without hesitation, he slammed his fist into the narrow glass window beside the door, reached through the jagged opening, ignoring the sting of glass slicing his hand, as he popped the lock. He saw the weakness in the facility and the camera placement from his last visit.

As he stepped inside, Lockland glanced down. Blood pooled in the grooves of his fingers, dripping onto the floor in slow, deliberate drops. He exhaled and pushed forward.

Once deeper inside, he stopped at a door near the end of the hallway. For a moment, he hesitated, his hand hovering over the knob. Then, with a deep breath, he turned it and entered.

Before him, in the center of the room, rested a new mahogany casket adorned with gold trimming. The polished surface reflected the soft light filtering through the windows.

Cakes' new resting place.

His gaze fell on a single chair in the corner, and he dragged it across the room until it sat directly in front of the casket. Slowly, he sank into the seat, resting his elbows on his knees while staring at the coffin.

He sighed, the sound heavy with frustration and guilt. This wasn't how it was supposed to be, but Lockland was a man of his word.

And he had promises to keep.

There was no way he could bury her, until he found Jalen.

The minutes passed in silence when headlights cut through the window, their beams slicing across the room and landing on his face.

A few minutes later, the sound of footsteps over shattered glass sliced the quiet. The Dust Boys entered the room, their silhouettes dark against the doorway's light.

"Are you sure about this?" Wakes asked.

Lockland turned his head slowly to face him, his dark eyes shrill and unwavering. He didn't say a word.

With silence as the speaker, the Dust Boys exchanged a look all knowing he was dead ass. So, together, they lifted the casket's lid and with slow, deliberate movements, raised his mother out.

Seeing her lifeless body stuck at his soul.

He sat there, rooted in place by the weight of his guilt. It pressed down on him, heavy and suffocating, pinning him to the chair. Only when he could move, he stood up sluggishly and followed them out the door.

The Dust Boys moved slowly, gently carrying Cakes' lifeless body through the doors of the house, washed in the soft glow of the moonlight. The faint creak of the floorboards under their steps was steady as Wakes led the way.

Lockland followed a few feet behind, blood from his earlier injury seeped through his bandaged hand, but he didn't seem to notice.

Still they continued and maneuvered the body carefully through the narrow hallway, the weight of their task pressing on their shoulders as much as the physical burden.

When they reached her room, Wakes pushed the door open with his foot. Things were exactly as Cakes had left them except the bed was made by Lockland.

They moved in unison, gently lowering Cakes' body onto the mattress, the springs creaked softly under her. With respect for the dead, they arranged her carefully, smoothing the edges of her dress and placing her hands neatly across her chest. For a second, they stood there, their eyes lingering on her as if she might wake up at any moment.

Finally, Wakes broke the silence. “You good, Lock?”

He nodded once.

Dion opened his mouth to speak but Wakes shook his head no. And so, one by one, they filed out of the room, their footsteps muffled against the old carpet.

When the house was silent again, Lockland stepped inside, his boots barely made a sound as he crossed to the bed. For a few minutes, he just stood there, his hands hanging at his sides, his bare chest rising and falling.

He reached down, taking the edge of the quilt and pulling it up to her chin, just as she used to do for him when he was a boy. His fingers brushed against the fabric, the familiar texture sparking a rush of memories.

Her laughter.

Her love.

“You’re home now,” he whispered. “I know you ain’t see it like this. But I’ma need a little more time.”

With one last look, he turned and walked out of the room, pulling the door closed softly behind him.

Outside, the Dust Boys waited by the car, their eyes turning to him as he stepped onto the porch. They didn't speak, but the heft of their worry hung in the air. Lockland didn't acknowledge any of them. He just walked past them, and toward the car, removing a blunt from his pocket.

Once everyone was tucked in the vehicle he sighed deeply. "First he fucked with my mother's casket, then he shot up the truck, next he called Shannon and fucked with her about...about Asia."

They didn't know that part.

"I need to find my sister, y'all. Before he do something else, and I just start shooting at random."

Wakes pulled off, while every other nigga ducked slightly.

Davis sat slouched in his car, the orange glow of his cigarette illuminating his face. The stench of tobacco and fast food caused the place to stank up.

Hours had passed since he'd left Memory alone in the apartment, but he didn't care. Instead of checking on her, he'd spent the evening laughing with his friends, blowing the rest of the money she'd given him, claiming he needed to get them some more food.

It was always about food, but he never brought any for her when he returned.

Now, as he sat parked outside the run-down building he reluctantly called home, he finally decided it was time to head inside. He hoped Memory had done what he hadn't ever...finish cleaning his place. He was just about to bounce when Jalen slid into the seat beside him.

As if the piece of shit belonged to him, he leaned back, his hands casually buried in his jacket pockets, his dark eyes scanning the street outside.

Davis froze, his fingers tightening on the steering wheel. "I know you," he said, his voice shaky.

Jalen chuckled, a low, humorless sound. "Why wouldn't you? You fucking my sister."

"What you want with me?" Davis asked, his voice laced with fear. "I ain't hurt her if that's what you think."

Jalen glared. "I don't give a fuck about that bitch."

"But she your sister."

"And, lil nigga? What's blood if it don't stand for nothing?"

Davis hesitated, his mind racing. "So...so what do you want then?"

I need you to do something for me," Jalen said smoothly, his voice calm but carrying an edge that made Davis's skin crawl. "If you do it right, I'll make sure you get enough money to get out of this dump you call home." He gestured vaguely at the surrounding buildings. "Why would you even live in a place like this anyway? Everywhere I look, is trash."

Davis' face burned with shame, but he forced himself to stay composed. The gag was at one point Jalen lived in a sewer, so he should talk.

Moving on, Jalen reached into his pocket and pulled out a thick wad of cash. He peeled off four crisp hundred-dollar bills and held them out. The sight of the money made Davis' heart race. It was more cash than he'd seen in his life.

And then suddenly he thought about his payday.

"I hope you not trying to take my good thing away," Davis said, trying to sound tough as he took the money. "She's coming into some cash soon, and half of it is mine."

Jalen's expression darkened.

"Here's the deal," Jalen said coldly, his voice like steel. "You gonna follow my instructions to the letter. Or go against me and die."

Inside the apartment, Memory had just hung up the phone after a brief, reluctant conversation with her older brother, Turner. His voice was slurred, his words erratic. He was high, again, and talking to him had left her feeling drained. She sighed heavily and set her phone down on the table.

When the door opened, her mood shifted instantly. Davis walked in, and she ran to him, wrapping her arms around his neck. The smell of cigarettes and cheap cologne clung to him, but she didn't care. "I missed you so much," she said, burying her face in his chest. "I thought you weren't coming back."

"Why would I do that, pretty girl?" Davis replied smoothly, pressing a kiss to her forehead. "You know I love you."

Her cheeks flushed, and she pulled back slightly. "Where's the food?"

Davis winced, feigning regret. "Sorry, babe," he said, his voice dripping with false sincerity. "The streets got in the way, and I forgot to pick something up. But if you want, we can go get something now."

Memory shook her head. "I don't really have an appetite," she admitted softly.

Davis seized the opportunity to change the subject. "Listen, I want you to get in contact with Lockland."

She frowned. "My brother? I thought you didn't like him."

"I never said that," Davis replied, his tone carefully measured. Lip slightly bubbled from their last interaction. "I just don't like how he acts like he's your father sometimes."

"So why do you want me to see him?" She asked, her suspicion clear.

"Because he needs to know you're okay. The way I took you out of there was wrong. Just meet up with him and let him know you good. Besides, I don't want your brother coming around here looking for me. You know how crazy he is."

Memory nodded slowly, understanding the unspoken truth in his words. "Alright," she said. "He been calling me like he's losing it, so I'll go see him tonight."

Davis smiled, his charm back in full force. "That's my girl."

It was two o'clock in the morning when Memory called Lockland. For real it didn't matter how late or early it was because at the end of the day, he would always run to his little sister if she needed him. Pulling into the empty parking lot of a grocery store, he waited impatiently for her to appear.

Where was she?

Finally Memory slid into the passenger seat, her arms crossed over her chest. It was giving big attitude even though she was still cute. Lockland glanced at her, his hands gripping the wheel tightly.

For a beat he wrestled with what to say. A part of him wanted to remind her that just because their mother was gone didn't mean she was free of him. But another part, the brotherly part, wanted to chill and just listen.

To make sure she was good.

"Where are you?" He asked in a low tone.

"What you talking about? I'm here." She replied, arms still crossed.

"I mean, where you staying now?"

"I'm staying with Davis, Lockland. I know you know that."

Actually, he didn't. He had hoped she was smart enough to avoid making such a mistake, but her response confirmed what he feared.

She was still stupid as fuck.

"It's like this...ma wanted me to take care of you," he said, his tone softening slightly. "She told me to promise her—"

"That's a lie."

He glared. "I wouldn't play like that about Cakes. You know me. She really did ask me to look after you. And if you let me, I will."

The pain bubbled in her gut. "Then how come she never said it to me?"

"Because she wasn't the same. You saw her, Memory. But when she could speak, and remember, she remembered you."

"You know you don't gotta do this no more, right?"

"What you mean?"

"She's gone. You can go back to the life you had before she died. You not even blood."

Lockland's temper flared. "And you think that matters? I still care about you."

"Stop being fake. You can just leave me alone if you don't wanna be bothered, Lockland."

One of the problems he felt she had was that she didn't know what to say out her mouth. He was about to check her, when a movement outside caught his eye. A man was running toward the car, a gun glinting in his hand under the streetlights.

"I know this nigga not crazy."

Lockland reacted instantly, slamming the car into drive as bullets shattered the quiet night. The distinct cracks of gunfire echoed in the parking lot, as Memory's panicked screams lit up the car.

Lockland swerved, as he maneuvered to avoid the attacker's shots. Remembering he wasn't without power himself, he reached for the weapon tucked into his pocket and fired back, the recoil jolting his arm.

But when Memory screamed again, he realized he couldn't risk her safety. Had it just been himself he was willing to do whatever. Load, unload and reload for all he gave a fuck. Unfortunately, she was with him and so, he peeled out of the parking lot, tires screeching as they fled the chaos.

When they were alone again, parked on a quiet side street, Lockland did his best to calm down. He stared straight ahead, his chest rising and falling, before finally turning to Memory.

"Did you set me up?" He asked, his voice cold and steady.

"Me?! I wouldn't do that shit!" She insisted.

"Don't lie to me," he yelled.

"I'm being honest! I really wanted to see you!" She cried, tears streaming down her face. "I...I was missing you and figured this was a good time to see you again."

"Why?" He questioned, suspicion cutting deeper than his words.

"Because I left without telling you," she said, her voice trembling. "So...so I wanted to explain."

"What happened right before you called me?"

"I don't understand—"

"I'm asking you a simple question!"

She thought about what she was doing before and then nodded when the memory came flooding back. "I was cleaning the house. And...and then Turner called."

Lockland's sighed, knowing that he told him to tell her to reach out. But what he didn't do was confirm that he told her to do so.

"I wasn't going to because I was still kinda mad, but then Davis convinced me. He wanted me to talk to you."

"So it was Davis' idea?"

"Please don't be mad at him."

"It doesn't matter. I'm taking you where you rest your head."

"Davis said he'd pick me up at the—"

"I said, I'm taking you!" He snapped, his voice leaving no room for argument. "And trust me, you don't want to fuck with me right now."

Turner walked briskly down the street, the smell of exhaust lingering in the air from a passing car.

The night was unusually quiet.

He was on his way to a friend's house. A person who always had a pill to pop or something to drink, when suddenly, the screech of tires shattered the stillness.

In a fucking hurry, a black van pulled alongside him, its sliding door whipping open before he could react. Before Turner could wobble run for dear life, rough hands yanked him inside, slamming the door shut.

Turner hit the cargo van's hard, bare floor, pain shooting up his spine.

His head throbbed as he tried to sit up, but what he saw next made his heart plummet. Lockland sat across from him, on the floor, knees pulled up, his expression cold.

Beside him was Dion who looked ready to crack the man's jaw.

"I need you to tell me something," Lockland said, his voice calm. "And I need you to be clear."

Turner glared at him, trying to mask his fear. "You gonna have to stop snatching me like this. I'm not scared of you, nigga."

"Stop talking before I push your nose to the back of your skull," Lockland said, cutting him off mid-sentence. "When you went to that ambulance the other day, what was the reason?"

"I didn't park next to no ambulance," Turner said quickly.

"I didn't say 'park.' I said 'went,'" Lockland replied smoothly. "No need in lying. Tell the truth and save yourself."

Turner's shoulders slumped as the weight of being caught pressed down on him. He felt stupid.

Exposed.

"What were you doing next to that ambulance?" Lockland demanded.

"You not gonna hurt me," Turner said, bravely. "You all about family remember?"

"He might not," Dion interjected, his voice low and dangerous. "But we all know I will."

Turner flinched at the sound of Dion cracking his knuckles.

"Jalen lives in the van," Turner finally admitted, his voice barely above a whisper. "I mean...ambulance."

Lockland raised an eyebrow. "Lives in an ambulance? You sound crazy."

"I'm telling you, that's the truth."

"Where he park that bitch?" Lockland pressed.

"Anywhere he wants to. That's the whole purpose. You'll never be able to find him."

"I won't be able to find him," Lockland said, his voice dropping into a deadly calm. "But you will."

Turner's head whipped side to side, panic flooding his face. "Please don't make me. He's still my brother and—."

"The days of 'please' were over when that nigga tried to kill me. And you chose a side. So if you don't lead me to him, you're an enemy to me. Maybe even worse."

Turner opened his mouth to argue, but Lockland kept going.

"He almost killed me with Memory in the car. Now I know you don't give a fuck about me, but do you got any love for her?"

"I can't do it, man. My mother loved you, but that nigga my real brother."

He was useless so he wanted to show him how much. Lockland stood up, grabbed his pistol and knocked him across the face several times until he passed out.

When he was done he looked up at the Dust Boys. "Drop this nigga off on the curb and take me to that bitch house."

The new Yukon glistened under the moonlight, its sleek black paint reflecting the faint glow. Wakes was posted behind the wheel, his dreadlocks brushing his shoulders as he adjusted the rearview mirror. Dion sat to his right, his fingers tapping lightly on the window.

In the back, Shoes was hunched forward, as Lockland sat beside him, his dark eyes fixed on the house across the street. Through the large front window, he could see movement between the slits of the blinds. Lockland believed the yellow bone who was kissing on a Persian cat was out of his league, but whatever.

“Wakes,” Lockland said, his voice low but steady. “You sure this the chick?”

Wakes didn’t look back. He nodded once. “That’s his bitch.”

Lockland shifted in his seat, the chain around his neck sparkled briefly as it caught the street’s light.

Shoes looked toward him. "Want me to snatch her?"

TWO BLOCKS AWAY

Jalen's fists were clutched in his lap as he sat in the passenger's seat of Everett's truck.

He had gotten word that Breanna was with another nigga and had intentions on killing him that night. Instead he was looking at his former foster brother who was propped outside.

His jaw clenched as he leaned forward, his breath fogging the window. He could see Lockland through the tinted glass, sitting calmly in the backseat like he had all the time in the world.

Everett glanced over, his hands loosely gripping the wheel. "You want me to hit him?" He asked, his tone lazy, like he was asking what they should eat for dinner. "Because it ain't about nothing. We could end this tonight."

Jalen shook his head, his teeth grinding audibly. "Nah," he said, his voice cold. "Can't take the chance of Breanna getting hurt. Or her thinking I brought heat to her door."

Everett raised an eyebrow but didn't push. He reached for a cigarette from the dash, lighting it with a quick flick before rolling the window down slightly to let the smoke out. "You got somethin' else in mind then?"

Jalen's eyes narrowed as he leaned back into his seat, his breathing slow and deliberate. "Yeah. Since he so worried about my bitch, let me go fuck with his."

The neighborhood was quiet, the kind of quiet that felt wrong.

Jalen and Everett stood in front of Cakes' house. Jalen's dark eyes scanned the windows, before he glanced at Everett.

"You sure about this?" Everett whispered.

"Just open the door." He didn't care who saw him. Hell, he *wanted* someone to see him so that word could get back to Lockland.

Moving toward the backdoor, with what he did best and a few clicks, Everett had gained entry, and the door creaked open. He slipped inside first, his movements smooth and practiced.

Jalen followed.

His pace deliberate, his eyes scanning the living room as if daring a nigga to say something. He might not have liked or loved her, but at the end of the day she was still his mother. He even made sure to pause for a moment near the window, the curtains half-drawn. If anyone was watching from the street, they'd know he was there.

It didn't take long before they found Ms. Cakes in the bedroom. Her frail body was lifeless, her gray hair still neatly combed as if she'd just been sitting in her chair. Jalen stared down at her for a long moment, his jaw tightening.

"The rumor was true. This nigga really kept her here, huh?" Everett said. "That nigga is sadistic."

Jalen didn't respond.

For some reason her being there made him even more jealous. How could he love her more than he did?

Jalen bent down, his hands steady, and helped Everett lift her body.

It took them five minutes to move her. Five long, quiet minutes filled with nothing but the creak of the floorboards as they wrapped her in a blanket and carried her out the front door.

Her small frame sagging between them as they navigated the porch steps.

When Everett pushed a button to open the trunk, they lowered her inside and shut it without another word. Jalen wiped his hands on his jeans before sliding into the passenger seat.

"I can't believe it," Jalen whispered. "He really kept the body in the house."

Everett climbed into the driver's seat, the engine rumbling to life. He hesitated once and then said, "He gonna snap if he comes back and she's gone."

Jalen turned to him and glared. "Like I give a fuck."

Everett didn't say anything else. He shifted into gear, the tires crunching softly against the gravel as they pulled away from the house.

Jalen claimed he wanted word to get back to Lockland that he took Cakes, and so word did.

But what came next he was not prepared for.

Lockland, high most of the time and running on fumes of rage, went on a spree that left people terrified. For twenty-four hours straight, anyone associated with Jalen, in any capacity, past or present, received a visit from a man who many claimed was a lunatic. They heard of the body he supposedly kept to prevent from being buried.

Although lies, the things most said he did to her were atrocious. Some said he sucked on her titty like a baby. A few said he slept with her every night. One person claimed he ate her flesh.

And still, Lockland didn't care.

He wanted Cakes' body back, and he was willing to burn Baltimore to get it.

The first stop was Jalen's barber. The man barely had time to react before Lockland and the Dust Boys stormed into the shop.

"Who the fuck are—."

His words were halted in his mouth as The Dust Boys fists beat him so badly, he ended up in the hospital. The thing was, the man hadn't seen him in weeks.

Next was Jalen's weed dealer, but she wasn't home. Lucky for her, the Dust Boys moved on without causing trouble.

The spree continued as Lockland took the beef to old friends Jalen grew up with. Most had moved out of town, but the two who stayed behind weren't so fortunate. One had their car smashed beyond recognition by the Dust Boys, glass crunching under Lockland's boots as he walked away with a grin on his face.

Twenty people had been touched in some way and still Lockland wanted to touch more.

It wasn't just about finding Jalen at this point.

It was about causing so much shit that people were hitting Jalen up directly. Telling him that whatever he was involved in, he had better leave them out of it.

Still, Jalen would not return the body, that still sat in Everett's trunk, to its resting place.

Lockland wasn't done.

Shit hit the fan when Breanna's cat became the unwitting catalyst that shifted the battle. Breanna, who had narrowly avoided Lockland's visit by sheer chance, found herself in Jalen's arms, crying gold digger's tears. She was in his ambulance, a place she hated to be. Everett and Tink were in the cramped space also.

She was there not because of love, but because her cat, had been taken. The house had been broken into, furniture overturned, but it was the missing cat that left her in pieces.

Through loud sobs the cold-hearted monster said, "I'm gonna die if I don't get him back! Do you hear me? I *need* him back!"

Jalen held her awkwardly. "We gonna find him."

"Don't fucking lie to me! How could you say that when you don't even know where he is or who has him?" He knew. But he couldn't tell her or she would never let him suck on that cute pussy again.

Before he could respond, his phone buzzed. He looked at Tink who said, "I got her," as he peeled himself off her body.

Doing the most, she now cried in Tink's arms.

Walking into the bathroom he answered, "Who is this?"

Lockland's voice was low and dangerous. "Be lucky she wasn't home."

"Fuck is wrong with—."

"Listen, nigga, you dead for what you did to me. To my family. So let's be clear, you gonna die anyway. Now if you don't bring her back, I'll drag Breanna in this too. You have four hours because at this point, I don't give a fuck anymore."

"How I know you won't kill me if I do?"

"You don't."

When Lockland returned to Cakes' house, and stepped into her bedroom, she was lying in her bed, just as if she'd never left.

His expression didn't soften as he removed a blunt from his pocket and lit it, inhaling deeply before exhaling. His eyes were red, his knuckles and bare chest blood splattered from fighting and causing havoc.

The Dust Boys stood in the hallway their expressions intense. They weren't sure what scared them more. The fact that Cakes' body was back or the wild look in Lockland's bloodshot eyes.

He turned to them, his voice calm. "Let's pick up Turner again. This time, he won't have a choice but to help."

Lockland didn't return the cat and Jalen was furious.

As he leaned against the wall of his ambulance, the subtle hum of the engine vibrating beneath him, all he wanted was to kill his ass. In the small bed behind him, Breanna was fast asleep, her soft breathing the only sound in the cramped space.

He hated how much he wanted this girl and didn't want the risk of her finding out how crazy Lockland actually was. He needed him dead like yesterday so he could fake control and maintain his even faker life.

Pulling out his phone, he dialed Grace's number, his hands trembling slightly as he pressed it to his ear. When she picked up, her voice was calm, almost amused.

"What's the status?" He whispered. "You have to kill Lockland *now,* or I swear I'll kill you instead."

"It's not that simple. He's hard to catch, and honestly? The stories I've been hearing on the streets about him..." She hesitated. "Let's just say, if you want him dead, you're gonna need to pay me more. A lot more."

Jalen's jaw tightened, his knuckles white as he gripped the phone. "I already gave you more, bitch. Don't fuck with me. Get this nigga now. Or else."

CHAPTER ELEVEN

Turner sat slouched on the edge of his porch, the faint smell of cigarette smoke lingering around him. The creak of tires on gravel pulled his attention, and he looked up just as the black Yukon rolled to a stop in front of his house. The Dust Boys were here, and Turner already knew what that meant.

He shook his head.

He was done fighting.

Lockland had already fucked him up and so he couldn't take no more smackdowns.

The passenger door opened, and Dion stepped out, his face blank but his eyes serious. Turner sighed heavily, rubbing a hand over his face as he rose. His knees ached, and his stomach churned. Raising his hands slowly, he tried for a shaky grin that didn't land.

"Look," he said, "I'm not even high. I'm good. I'm willing to help, alright? Just...just don't hurt me no more."

Dion walked to the back door, opened it, and motioned for Turner to get inside.

Turner hesitated for a split second before stepping off the porch, his hands still in the air as he walked toward the car. The cold air bit at his skin until he slid inside. Now all he felt was heat and tension.

Lockland sat to his left, silent and still. Turner swallowed hard, his throat dry as sandpaper. Dion climbed in on his right, shutting the door behind him with a dull *thunk*.

"All this shit over, mama?" Turner asked. "Do this make sense to you?"

Silence.

"So you really gonna do this, huh?" Turner asked. "You really done with Jalen?"

From the driver's seat, Wakes shook his head slowly, put the truck into gear and pulled off.

Lockland was on his third blunt and looking crazier than ever.

The truck containing the Dust Boys and Lockland, sped down the empty stretch of road, the headlights cutting through the thick darkness. Turner was also still inside, his body reeking from an overall funk. The hum of the engine was the only consistent sound. Dion leaned forward from the backseat, his broad shoulders nearly pressing against the headrests.

After getting intel from Turner and making a few calls, to Dion it looked like they were gonna put both Jalen and Cakes to rest. "We got him this time! I can feel that shit, man. This is it."

Lockland held a blunt loosely from his fingers. His eyes were locked on the road ahead, his expression blank, because his mind contained crazy thoughts.

But he had an audience.

Because in the backseat, Wakes watched him carefully. Unable to take much more, he leaned over to Shoes, who was now behind the wheel.

"Pull over," Wakes said firmly.

Shoes glanced at him, then back at the road. "Lock didn't say pull over so I'ma keep pushing."

"I don't care what he said, nigga," Wakes snapped. "Look at him. He's high as fuck and not thinking straight. Pull the fuck over! Now!"

Shoes hesitated, his hands tightening on the wheel. Lockland caught the exchange and finally gave a slight nod, his eyes narrowing at Wakes as the vehicle slowed on the gravel shoulder.

The truck hadn't fully stopped before Wakes flung the door open and stepped out, his boots crunching against the gravel. He walked around to the back passenger side and yanked the door open, the cool night air rushing inside.

"What you doing, Lock?" Wakes demanded his voice agitated. "I mean for real. You smoking without knowing if we about to walk into a trap."

Lockland's eyes narrowed as he put the blunt out. "I'm good. If anybody overthinking it's you."

"Listen, I know you fucked up about the past twenty-four hours," Wakes responded. "But I think we should pause on this tip Turner gave us. Because this...all of it... doesn't feel right. He been lowkey sabotaging from the gate."

"But he be knowing where he at too."

"I don't trust tonight. The nigga was just sitting on the porch, waiting? It don't add up!"

Lockland climbed out the truck, his movements slow and deliberate. He stood toe-to-toe with Wakes, his posture imposing. "Who in charge?"

Wakes didn't back down. "You are. But if you want us to walk into—"

"If it's me...then let it be me. Because if you don't trust me, you can leave. Nobody keeping you here, man."

Wakes' voice softened. "I'll never leave you, Lock. You know that. But I need you to fall back just for a second. You have—."

"Fall in line. I won't say it again."

For a moment, the two men stared each other down. Finally, Wakes feeling his friend's pain, stepped back, his shoulders stiff with frustration. "Fine. But don't say I didn't warn you."

Back in the truck, once they reached the ambulance, Turner's trembling hand pointed it out. The vehicle sat under the cover of an old overpass, its rusting exterior blending into the shadows. Lockland and the Dust Boys piled out, every man ready for war.

"There it is," Turner said, his voice shaky. "Told y'all niggas I knew where to go."

"Stay here," Lockland said as he moved forward with Dion, Wakes, and Shoes.

Wakes grabbed Lockland's arm. The more he looked at the scene, the more it appeared like a set up perfectly for them. "This doesn't feel right. Let's think this through."

Lockland shook him off. "We been thinking for too long, nigga. It's now or never!"

The four of them approached the ambulance, their footsteps muffled by the dirt. Lockland motioned for Shoes to check the back of the Ambulance while he and Dion moved to the front. Wakes lingered near the edge, watching the perimeter, his gut screaming at him to stop him and his family from being an easy mark.

But Lockland wouldn't hear of it.

As Lockland peered on the driver's side door, he noticed the lock was raised. "It's open," he whispered.

Suddenly Turner took off running.

Wakes, seeing this turned to Lockland and yelled, "Don't open the fucking—"

BOOM!

It was too late.

When Lockland pulled the driver's door, the van exploded.

The deafening roar shattered the night, the force of the blast throwing them backward like rag dolls. Flames erupted into the sky, the heat searing their skin even as they hit the ground. The smell of burning metal and rubber filled the air, along with the faint stench of charred flesh.

Lockland's ears rang as he staggered to his feet, his body aching from the impact. He looked around, panic setting in as he saw Wakes and Dion on the ground, coughing but alive.

But where was Shoes?

"Shoes!" Lockland yelled, his voice hoarse.

He tried to run to the flames, but Wakes caught him and flung him away, injuring his elbow in the process. As the ambulance burned, Lockland's heart sank as he stared at the inferno, the realization that all this shit was his fault.

Shoes was inside.

He had died.

And to make matters worse, he saw Grace pulling away from the scene.

The interior of the cargo container was dark, and a single, flickering bulb hung from the ceiling, casting shadows over the faces of the three men inside.

Jalen paced back and forth, his boots pressing against the steel floor as his fists were clenched.

Shit had truly hit the fan.

He knew it was a matter of time before the two men warred, but he hadn't realized it would get so intense.

As Jalen paced, Tink leaned against the wall, twirling a knife between his fingers, the blade catching the dim light with each spin. Everett, on the other hand, sat nearby on a crate, his massive arms crossed over his chest, his gaze fixed on Jalen.

"He actually tried to kill me." Jalen whispered, his voice reverberating through the container. He stopped pacing and slammed a fist into the wall, the impact echoing loudly.

"But you tried to hit him too," Everett announced.

"I don't give a fuck. You don't try and hit me!"

Everett looked at Tink to see if he also thought he sounded dumb. He was playing the victim when it was all his fault. Even from the beginning before Jalen crossed the line, the man tried to mend fences.

"If my dopehead brother hadn't picked sides and chose me time after time, I'd be dead right now."

Tink put the knife in his pocket and said, "So what you wanna do?"

Jalen turned to him, his glare so intense that Tink almost stepped back. "I was nice last time. But if he wanna see blood I'll show him gallons."

The silence that followed was heavy as Tink nodded slowly. "About time we stopped fucking with these niggas."

Everett unfolded his arms and rose. "As long as we smart, I'm good with whatever."

"It ain't about being smart no more," Jalen said. "It's about being savages, and I already got something in motion."

CHAPTER TWELVE

Davis and Memory walked side by side down the busy block. His arm draped lazily over her shoulder, a move that was more about control than affection. The sun hung high, its warm glow putting a little heat on the crisp air of the city. As they moved, Memory glanced down, her heart heavy despite the beauty of the day.

The plan was to go see a movie.

But Davis dangled a good time in front of her on countless occasions. So who knew what was under his sleeve now. When they made a slight detour she was shocked. The theater was conveniently located in the mall, but Davis had other plans.

"I can't wait to make you my wife."

She nodded.

"Like we really gonna live the good life."

She nodded again.

Finally he knew his charms were falling flat. When he glanced at her, he caught the sadness lingering in her eyes.

"What's wrong now?" He asked, his tone stern.

Memory hesitated, her voice soft. "I don't know. I just feel...bad."

"About what? Your mother dying. I mean you on that shit again? Because look, she's dead already. So let it the fuck go."

"It would be easier if we could bury her but—."

"Blame your brother 'cause that nigga Lockland on some other shit." He said. "I heard he got her posted up at the house and everything."

"That's a lie."

"Well at least she put you on the policy. That way you can—."

"I'm not on the policy," she admitted.

"Wait...what?"

"I found out she left everything for Lockland. I guess to make sure I didn't spend it all on stuff." She looked away. "Like you."

"So who been giving you money?"

"Lockland been putting cash in the ATM for me."

"So you expect me to take care of you and shit?"

His words struck like a physical blow, causing her stomach to twist painfully. It took everything in her to fight back the tears. And so, she stared at him, the beginnings of second thoughts creeping into her mind.

She had them before.

Sure.

But this time was different.

She didn't know where to turn. Her mother had been sick for so much of her life, growing weaker with each passing year that she didn't have the chance to teach her the ways of man. And now, here Memory was, falling victim to a nigga with a big smile, a big dick, and a heart as dark as space.

"I don't like how you talk to me sometimes," she said, her voice trembling.

"There we go," Davis said, throwing his hands up. "I always tell you, Memory, if you're gonna be my girl—."

"Maybe I shouldn't be though."

Now it was he who felt ill. The last thing he needed was to lose his meal ticket.

"Listen, I'm sorry if I don't talk to you the way you want," Davis said, his tone softening just enough to make her doubt her feelings. "But don't worry. All of that will change."

"You keep saying that. But when?"

"When you understand that everything I say doesn't mean I don't care about you," he replied smoothly, pulling her closer. "Some stuff just be about that tougher love."

She was tiring already of fighting. "Okay, so where do we go from here?"

"We gonna go into this mall, grab something to eat, watch a movie, and have a good time." He kissed her lips. Suddenly he released her and slapped at his pockets.

"What's wrong?"

"Do me a favor first."

"What?"

"Let's stop by the ATM. I left my wallet at home."

Memory's stomach dropped, the familiar sensation of dread washing over her. "And then what?"

"Call your brother again. If he gonna be cashing you out, he gonna know I'm good for it."

She stopped walking, her feet planting firmly on the ground as fear coursed through her. "I told you that he doesn't want to see me right now because he believes I set him up."

"But you didn't."

"He still don't believe me! Fuck! I'm sick of your broke ass begging and asking for money! Shut the fuck up and listen! For once! The dick been trash, you don't wanna do nothing but lay on the floor and you sound dumb some of the times when you be talking about doing shit with money you don't got!"

Davis farted.

She went on him so hard he had to start all over.

"I'm sorry. It's just that I was gonna ask you to marry me tomorrow okay? And I wanted to make sure it was cool with him. There you go!"

Her eyes widened. "Oh my, God! I'm sorry! I didn't know!"

Just that quick he was back in control. "I know! Because you don't trust me, and I swear that shit hurts! Maybe I shouldn't ask you to marry me now."

"No! Don't say that!" Her entire body trembled. "I'll do it! I'll do it!"

"That's my girl."

Broke niggas 1.

Stupid girls 0.

CHAPTER THIRTEEN

Lockland stood on top of a car at night in a parking lot.

He was trying to get a good look of a certain vehicle.

Once he saw what he wanted, he hopped down and walked in front of Grace's apartment building, where her vehicle was posted. She didn't know he was there, but she would find out soon enough.

As she left the building, digging through her pocketbook, she quickly realized why it was always better to keep your eyes forward and alert when moving about in the world.

"Let me talk to you for a moment," Lockland said as he approached her from behind.

Her heart skipped a beat because she hadn't seen him coming. The false sense of safety had her fucked up. "Actually, I was on my way to—."

"I don't give a fuck," he interrupted firmly, leaving no room for argument. "Not until you can tell me why you been following me."

Grace took a deep breath. "You already know. I have to keep an eye on you. And to be honest, I'm not even a hundred percent sure what I saw." She inhaled deeply. "But I'm glad to know you okay."

He stared at her for what seemed like forever. "What *did* you see though?"

She looked down and then out and then back at him. "Nothing...outside a vehicle blowing up."

"What details you want from me again? On my case."

"I don't have the paperwork on me."

"You better tell me something," he said, his voice carrying an unspoken threat.

"Can we go to my car?" She suggested, wanting to be closer to the weapon she had tucked on the side. Fuck the dumb shit. She had plans to blow him but now she was going to blow his brains out.

"Please, Lockland."

He started walking toward her vehicle, and she followed. Sliding into the passenger seat, he sat silently as she gripped the steering wheel. After a moment, she looked over at him and took another deep breath. Per usual, his hand hovered over the gun on his hip. While hers slid down to the compartment until he said, "Hands in your lap. I don't trust you."

Fuck. She thought to herself.

"What details do you want about that night?"

"Just more on what happened," she said cautiously, "My captain doesn't even know I'm watching you right now. And like I just said I don't have my notes."

"Well what does he think?"

"He thinks I can't find you."

He leaned back in his seat, tucking one hand in his pocket. Despite the danger behind his eyes, there was a sudden air of defeat around him that Grace hadn't seen before. It caught her off guard.

"I came up in hell…and I…I saw an opportunity to change my life. So I took it. Found someone who looked after me, loved me and I didn't care who I had to hurt to get it. And when she died," he said quietly. "I'm not a soft dude or—"

"I don't think you're soft just because you cared about your mother," she interrupted, her voice gentle. "In fact, I find it honorable."

"She wasn't my mother."

She frowned. "I don't understand."

"She's my foster mother. And when something went down, she chose me over her own son. And I always, I always thanked her for that. I always felt like I owed her. Like I didn't want her to think she made a mistake."

She looked forward, surprised by the revelation.

"If she chose you, that means she really loved you, Lockland. Why you think she did it?"

"Because her son...or her sons...are selfish ass niggas." He nodded slightly, not seeking validation but wanting to speak truth.

"Where your people?"

"I don't know...and I hope they never find me." He inhaled and exhaled. "Anyway, I gotta keep the promise I made. Don't make me go to darker places."

She gripped her hands in her lap as she noticed the gun he always touched on his hip was now out and sitting on his knee, barrel in her direction.

"What does that mean?"

"It means if you not on the up and up, Grace...if you not doing what you claim to be doing, giving me the time to close my loose ends...I gotta hurt you. You understand that right?"

She took a deep breath. "I do."

"Don't follow me again," he said firmly.

"Well, if that's the case," she sighed, "you gonna have to meet with me every night. That's the only way I'll back off. In other words, I'ma need updates. Starting tonight."

He nodded, pushing the door open. Before leaving, he leaned into the open window. "I'll see you at midnight. Stay safe."

"Stay alive."

The Dust Boys sat on the porch of Shoes' father's house, their presence heavy and dark. Lockland was with them, the atmosphere tense as they faced Shoes' grieving father. The news they'd just delivered hung in the air like a storm cloud.

Earlier in the evening the man's grief had exploded into violence, leaving the group battered as he took fists to his living room walls and their bodies. As a result, Lockland's nose bled, Wakes nursed a bruised eye, and Dion clutched his stomach.

But none of them...not a one made any attempts to fight him back.

"Find out who did this to my son," Larry said through gritted teeth, his voice breaking. "Deal with them and bring their dead body to me."

With that he stormed inside, slamming the door behind him.

As the Dust Boys sat quietly, Lockland's mind churned with the weight of another promise added to the pile already crushing him.

"I told you this," Wakes said suddenly, breaking the silence. "I told you I had a bad feeling, and you moved anyway, Lockland. And I need you to know, I blame you."

"You starting to get on my nerves, Yo," Dion responded, glaring at Wakes. "Like for real. I mean what you even talking about?"

"Fuck you mean what I'm talking about?"

"He didn't know what the fuck was going on. None of us did. That don't mean we not in this to the end. Together. And that means things don't always go as planned. Nobody wanted Shoes to die, but here we are."

Wakes took a deep breath, his frustration evident. At the same time, Dion was right. "What's the plan?" He asked, looking at Lockland. "Because I don't think I got it in me right now."

"I don't want nobody else hurt. So I'm gonna handle things by myself," Lockland said after a long pause.

"We not gonna let you do this," Wakes said.

"You already know you not gonna be able to get rid of me," Dion added. "So I don't know what the fuck you even talking 'bout right now."

"Lock, what did Jalen do to Asia?" Wakes said, believing that was another reason he was dead set on getting him. "What happened?"

Lockland sighed, his gaze fixed on his phone as a new message from Shannon lit up the screen. "Listen, stay out the way. I'll hit y'all later when I got Jalen's head."

When Shannon opened the door, Lockland was surprised by how clean her house was. She looked lighter, more at peace than she had in months. Normally she was in need of something...care...hugs...or sometimes just sex.

What had changed?

Now Lockland, he was another question.

When she saw his face she was stunned. Bruised face. Red eyes. It was just horrible and broke her heart. To make matters more intense, the moment he walked in, he begin pacing. Like his body was there but his mind was elsewhere.

She reached out to touch him, but he backed away. Normally he accepted her advances, so what changed?

"Did you want coffee?" She asked.

He shook his head. "Nah...but what's this about, Shannon?"

"Memory," she said, her voice careful. "I saw her at the mall with Davis and she looks stressed. More stressed than I've ever seen her before."

He frowned. "Why you concerned?"

"I know how dealing with things, or trying to deal with things fucks with you."

He shifted a little. "What's that supposed to mean?"

"Is your mother...is your mother at the house? Instead of the home."

Silence.

She stepped closer and he took the same amount of space back.

"Is she, baby? The streets are saying some wild things right now."

He took a deep breath. "I don't need you in the mix."

"You didn't have to tell me," she said simply. "We were together for years and had a...had a...daughter together. So—"

She paused, unable to say the words, but they both knew what she was feeling still burned. It burned bright for both of them. So bright not everybody knew what happened.

"Listen, I gotta go. I'll come back when—."

She grabbed his hand. "Please don't leave.

He shoved her back a little.

"Lockland...I know you're still in there." Shannon's voice trembled as she moved closer, one hand on his back. "And I know you spent your entire life trying to make things right with Jalen because you felt bad that Cakes chose you. But understand none of this was your fault."

Lockland turned to face her. "Of course it's my fault. Even what happened to our daughter."

"No it's not," she insisted. "You tried to reintroduce me to Jalen after learning what happened to him in that van and he used your love and guilt against you because that's what jealous ass niggas do. And then he—" She stopped, her stomach twisting with the memory.

Lockland reached out, but she pushed him away. "I have to deal with this at some point. And I don't want you to try to save me. I was wrong to put it on you in the first place. I just gotta...I just gotta let it burn."

Saying the words out loud seemed to lift a weight off her chest. "All I wanted to say is it wasn't your fault," she repeated, her voice steadier now. "But if you're gonna make it right, by putting that nigga down, let me be there for you by helping Memory."

"And what can I do for you?"

"I would love to see the look on his face when he learns he didn't break me. When he learns that I'm doing better. Right before you take his life."

ONE YEAR EARLIER

The park was quiet except for the occasional rustle of leaves in the breeze and the distant hum of cars. Lockland sat on the bench, a bottle of whiskey resting between his legs.

Jalen stood nearby, leaning against a tree, his phone glowing faintly in his hand as he scrolled absently. The penthouse lifestyle suited him...his clothes clean and sharp, his cologne light but expensive, lingering in the cool night air.

But his teeth were still yellow, and it was obvious he was very much bulimic.

They hadn't spoken in years before this, but now, after months of phone calls, they'd finally met in person. Shit felt off at first, but Jalen had been filling the silence with stories about his penthouse life and Breanna, the girl he claimed was his world. Lockland didn't know her, but he'd heard her name enough times to paint a picture.

More than anything, she cared about Jalen to hear Jalen tell it, so that made her good in his eyes.

"You ever wonder why I didn't wanna get in that van?" Jalen asked suddenly, his voice low and distant.

Lockland looked up, his brows furrowing. "I thought it was 'cause you panicked. And them niggas were chasing us." He knew the real story, that's why he felt bad, but he wanted Jalen to have the moment.

Jalen let out a dry chuckle, shaking his head.

He took a long pull from the bottle. "Nah, man, that wasn't it." He exhaled deeply. "The man in the van... I knew him. He'd been around before. Used to give me and some of the other kids candy for favors. To see our dicks and shit like that."

Lockland sat up straighter. "What you saying?"

Jalen's face twisted, pain flickering behind his eyes. "I'm saying he didn't just give us candy. Things got...wrong. And I never forgot." He looked over at Lockland, his expression unreadable. "That's why I didn't wanna get in. But there wasn't nowhere else to go."

The words hung in the air.

Lockland stared at his brother. "J," he said softly, his voice trembling. "I'm sorry you went through that shit, bro. Like for real. I didn't know... I...." He paused, his throat thick with guilt. "I never wanted to replace you. And after we fought, I hated you but when Turner told me what happened... and everything made sense I just had to find you. But I wanted time to mend things. Shit been fucking me up. Like the guilt...guilt is the one thing I can't get with."

Jalen nodded slowly. "So you did know?"

Damn.

He made a mistake.

"No worries...guilt always fucked with you, and you tried to make it right."

Lockland smiled. "I know...it's kinda like my kryptonite."

"I wish I gave a fuck that much. Because for real, Lockland, I don't be giving a fuck about nothing but Breanna sometimes."

For a moment, the tension seemed to ease.

"She's getting worse, you know," Lockland said, breaking the quiet.

Jalen's squinted. "Who?"

"Ma. Her mind's slipping more and more every day. Sometimes, I don't even think she knows who I am."

Jalen shifted, his jaw clenching. This question felt heavy. "Does she... does she ask about me?"

Lockland hesitated, looking down at the bottle in his hands. "I don't wanna lie to you, man," he said finally. "Nah, she doesn't. Her mind's too far gone."

Jalen's face hardened. With all hope lost, he forced a smile. "Figures. I'm not even tripping for real."

He straightened up, brushing off his jeans like he was shaking off the conversation. "What about you?" He asked, his tone lighter now, almost teasing. "Got a family?"

Lockland nodded. "Yeah. I'm still with Shannon.

"You lying," he said, jealousy filling his chest. How come they all chose him? "I still remember her posted up on the steps talking about being a good mother and having your baby."

"You remember that?"

"I remember everything."

"Well...I got a little girl named Asia. She's five now."

"Asia? That's ma's middle name."

"Yep," Lockland said proudly. "And Shannon is a good mother too. I just want...I just want her to have the best."

Jalen nodded. "Your girl and my niece, huh? You gotta introduce me sometime."

Lockland hesitated, but something in Jalen's tone sounded almost genuine. "Yeah," he said quietly. "I'd like that."

"Set it up," Jalen responded.

"I'll do that...maybe tomorrow. I'm taking her to the carnival."

"When?"

"Tonight."

The Carnival

The smell of popcorn and cotton candy filled the air. The colorful lights from the Ferris wheel reflected in Asia's wide eyes as she held her father's hand, skipping alongside him. Shannon walked on his other side, smiling as she watched their little girl tug at her cotton candy, the sugar sticking to her tiny fingers.

Lockland felt light for the first time in weeks. He wasn't thinking about the past, about his mother's worsening condition, or even about Jalen. This moment was perfect...just his family, together, enjoying the night.

But perfection doesn't last always.

Suddenly the sound of gunfire shattered the air, shrill and loud, cutting through the laughter like a blade. Lockland froze, his body tensing as he instinctively pulled Asia into his arms. He turned just in time to see Jalen step out from behind one of the carnival booths, his face twisted with rage, a gun in his hand.

"Jalen!" Lockland shouted, his voice breaking. "Please don't do this!"

Jalen didn't respond.

The gun went off again, the flash lighting his face for a brief moment. Lockland felt the impact before he understood what had happened. Asia's small body jerked in his arms, her cotton candy falling to the ground.

"NO!" Shannon screamed, her voice piercing into the crowd.

Lockland dropped to his knees, clutching Asia tightly, his hands slick with blood. Her eyes fluttered, her small lips parting as if she was trying to speak. But no words came.

Jalen stood there for a moment, his chest heaving, his hand trembling around the gun. Then he turned and disappeared into the chaos, the crowd screaming and scattering around him.

Lockland's world crumbled in that instant.

That was the moment something broke inside him.

From that night on, Lockland's life had one purpose: to find Jalen.

And he wouldn't stop until he was gone for good.

In hell, and away from everybody else he loved.

CHAPTER FOURTEEN

Lockland sat on the floor, his back resting against the cold wall. His mother's body was a shadowy outline in the dim room, barely visible in the darkness.

His head hung low, his chain brushed his bare chest. He hadn't moved much since coming back. His body ached, his muscles stiff from being thrown by the explosion, but none of it mattered.

Not the pain, not the silence.

Nothing.

Losing Shoes had torn something out of him. And talking to Shannon had left him hollow. And now, sitting here with nothing but the weight of the past pressing down on him, Lockland realized there were no heroes in this story.

They were all villains...every single one of them.

His mother, even her, had a part to play in all this chaos. She wasn't just a victim; she'd set the stage. A bunch of kids, lost and needing direction, had found only devastation instead because she wanted to save one person, knowing she was ill.

Memory.

At the end of the day did it matter?

Did Lockland care?

No.

Jalen had killed his daughter, friend and left his ex-girlfriend rocked.

He had to pay.

The thought settled in his chest like a stone, cold and unmoving. If he wanted to take Jalen out, it couldn't be the way he'd been doing things. He'd been chasing ghosts, fighting fire with fire, and losing everything along the way.

No more.

If this was going to end, he had to rethink every move, every step. He had to put his life on the line, and oddly enough, he was ready and willing to die.

Suddenly he felt a weird peace.

The smell of decay lingered in the living room, faint but unmistakable, seeping from the bedroom where their mother rested. Turner wrinkled his nose, shifting uncomfortably on the worn-out couch as he looked across at Lockland, who resembled a mad man. Despite the heavy air,

Lockland sat across from him, with an intense stare.

"So uh...is it true you got my mama in here?"

"You gonna do something for me," Lockland said ignoring his question, his voice low but firm.

"Why should I do anything else for you?"

"Because you tried to get your own brother killed."

Turner chuckled once. "You and I both know you not my brother."

"Fair enough." Lockland sat back, grabbed a blunt and struck it alive with a flame. "Well let's do it like this...I know you blaming yourself about ma. Been blaming yourself for a while."

Turner's laugh was snappy, bitter. "I don't know what you talking about. I'm not blaming myself for shit. It was the disease that took her out, not me."

Lockland's gaze hardened. "You been blaming yourself," he said, his voice rising slightly. "Because when she fell last year, you weren't here to help. And that caused her condition to get worse. A little after that, you went looking for your blood brother who you realize never gave a fuck about you. Seeking emotional connection from a demon." He paused. "Just like I did. The thing is...he don't give a fuck about none of us. And I honestly believe to hurt Cakes, he wants to kill you, me and even Memory."

Turner's jaw tightened, and he looked away, his body stiffening. "Not true."

"I swear it is, Turner. It's why he killed my daughter. Because she had...she had her middle name. That I told Shannon to give her." Guilt hit him again, but he pushed it away.

"You never told me—."

"But ma knew who the nigga really was, and she always tried to tell me."

Lockland rose, his towering presence commanded the room. Next he walked away and returned with a letter. "She wrote this to you when she was good. Wanted to put pen to paper before shit got worse."

Turner opened the sealed envelope and read each word. He saw Turner visually change, despite not knowing what the contents said. Whatever she penned, Turner was different. That much was evident.

Folding it up, he stood up, tucked it in his pocket and sat back in his seat.

"Jalen gotta go," Lockland said. "You know that. He's an emotional, jealous ass nigga. And right now that energy is turned to me and even you. Now I got a plan to find him, but I don't want it direct."

"What that mean?"

"I know you know where he is since he don't have that ambulance anymore. I need him found now."

Turner begin to pace, while scratching is uncombed hair.

"If you wanna make this right, you gonna help me. No more games. Be a man, T. For ma. Shit, for yourself."

At the liquor store, the clinking of bottles echoed off the cramped aisles as Tink browsed the shelves. He barely glanced up when Turner walked inside.

"Hey, man," Turner called out. "You buying something? You gonna get me something too?"

Tink looked at him in disgust. "Why would I do that?" He asked with disdain.

"Because it's about to be Thanksgiving."

"It's a month away."

"Same thing," Turner shot back. "Come on, man. Help a nigga out and shit."

For reasons even Tink couldn't explain, he relented, grabbing an extra bottle of vodka alongside his usual bottle of brown. He paid for it and handed it to Turner at the register, the clinking of change the only sound between them.

As they exited the store, Tink made a right while Turner bucked left. But just as Tink rounded the corner, he found himself face-to-face with Lockland.

"What you want?" Tink asked in direct fear of his life.

"I know about you and Breanna," Lockland said evenly. "I been at her house almost every night...and one of them nights...I saw you. And when I got closer, through the cracked blinds, I saw her riding your dick."

Tink's stomach dropped, and he felt the liquor bottle nearly slip from his grasp.

"I don't know what you—."

"No need in lying. I got pictures." He grabbed the folded velvet lint roller from his pocket and dusted his own pants. "That's foul, but I ain't gotta tell him all that. If you play along."

If this got out, how dangerous would Jalen be? He was sick over a female who wanted nothing to do with him.

"Don't worry," Lockland continued, his voice calm but menacing. He placed both hands on his chest. "I'm not gonna tell him. For now."

"Then why you stepping to me?" Tink asked, his voice shaky.

"Because I just want you to know that I know."

The sound of splashing water echoed through the indoor swimming pool. Everett emerged from his fourth lap, his muscles rippling as he climbed the ladder. As he wiped water from his face, he froze when he saw Lockland.

Waiting.

"What you doing here?" Everett asked, trying to remain calm.

"You gonna get out that pool, and you gonna come with me," Lockland said flatly.

"No, I'm not, either."

"I think you confused." Lockland chuckled, but there was no humor. "But I'm sure there's no need in me reminding you who I am. Now you can play games if you want, but it won't end well for you."

Everett's eyes flicked toward the exit, where three men stood...strangers with hard faces and intense eyes. They weren't the Dust Boys. These were savages who got their hands dirty for the right price.

Lockland preferred it that way actually.

After losing Shoes, the pain was too much. All that was left in him was revenge.

"Where you taking me?"

"Do me a favor. Don't ask no more fucking questions."

Everett hesitated for only a moment before stepping toward the exit. Lockland followed close behind.

CHAPTER FIFTEEN

Jalen was posted in the cramped, sparsely lit garage where his crew often gathered. The smell of motor oil and burnt rubber hung heavy in the air. They all lounged on mismatched furniture and crates as he leaned back in a folding chair, his boots propped up on a tire.

Across from him was Antonio, someone he rolled with out of necessity because he always had women around. He was sucking back a can of beer and burped with every sip. Annoying Jalen to no end.

Normally he would be with Tink and Everett, but they had been nowhere to be found.

"You know what's funny though?" Jalen began, his voice carrying over the group. "For years niggas thought Lockland was smarter than everybody. Turns out he's average at best."

A few of the men chuckled, but Antonio raised an eyebrow. "You gotta be careful when you underestimate people. Especially him. He might pop up on you outta nowhere."

"You gonna tell him where I'm at or something?"

"Me?" He pointed at himself. "I want nothing to do with that nigga. But word is he back on that grass and he want you bad as an inmate wants less time."

Laughter erupted around them, and Jalen's jaw tightened. He leaned forward, his cigarette burning dangerously close to his fingers. "You feeling yourself tonight. Just know that he ain't the only boogieman around here."

Antonio shrugged. "If you say so, J."

"All I'm saying if he couldn't find me in over a year how he gonna find me now?"

Before Antonio could respond, the distant sound of an engine caught everyone's attention. Heads turned toward the opening of the cargo unit; the faint rumble grew louder. Jalen straightened in his seat, his eyes piercing in the area of the sound.

A tow truck came into view, its frame unmistakable even through the haze of the overhead lights. It was the chunk of trash on the back that confused him.

It was his ambulance.

Half-burnt, its charred metal glinted under the streetlights, the once-white paint now scorched and blackened. Spray-painted across the side in jagged red letters were the words: YOU NOT A GHOST YET. BUT YOU WILL BE.

The Tow truck unlatched the mess and pulled off before Jalen's men could catch the driver. When they returned the laughter started low, a few chuckles here and there, until it grew louder.

"Damn, Jalen," Antonio said. "Guess you not as invisible as you think."

Jalen's face was hot with humiliation. For some reason, he wondered who told him where he was. So he burned eyes of rage toward the sides of his head.

"Hold up, I know you don't think this is me," Antonio said immediately. "Let us not forget you haven't been able to find Tink or Everett in days." He sipped his drink.

He was right, and this annoyed him even more.

It was time to think smarter. Because even though no one was in the ambulance, what if it was an ambush instead of a drop off? Jalen felt like it was a mental game on Lockland's part, and he wasn't feeling it one bit. He figured he wanted him to know that he was aware of where he was, and not necessarily kill him just yet.

First thing he had to do was move to another unit, in another part of town. Then he had to observe who knew where he was. The only people he could think of was Tink and Everett.

Surely they wouldn't be so foul.

Or could they?

The night was eerily quiet as moonlight filtered through branches.

Jalen stood near the center of the park, his posture stiff, his hands buried in the pockets of his dark jacket. The obvious scent of damp earth and freshly fallen leaves surrounded him. His gaze was fixed on the horizon as Turner rushed up the cracked path, his breath visible in the chill.

"Thanks for meeting me," he said, his voice shaky but determined.

"What you want?" Jalen asked flatly.

Turner stopped a few feet away, his hands shoved deep into his hoodie's pockets. "I know you been looking for Tink. And I wanted to show you something."

"How you know that, nigga?"

Turner fucked up.

"Oh...I forgot who told me. But look." He pulled out his phone.

Jalen's eyes narrowed as he studied Turner's agitated movements. "What is it?" He asked, his tone laced with suspicion.

"Just look."

Jalen frowned as he saw Tink standing with Lockland outside a liquor store on the video. To be disrespected by Lockland and have him take away yet another friend or somebody on his side, burned his soul.

"He was with that nigga like they were cool," Turner blurted out. "He got his hand on him and everything. Shame. If I was you, I wouldn't trust him." He paused. "But there is worse news."

"What's that?" Jalen was rumbling inside.

"He fucking Breanna." He showed him another video taken between the blinds.

Jalen's expression darkened even more, but Turner, lost in his own thoughts, didn't notice at first. It wasn't until Jalen clutched his stomach and staggered toward a nearby tree that Turner realized something was wrong. Jalen bent over and vomited, his body convulsing, but what unsettled Turner most was how Jalen tilted his head to the side, just enough to keep one eye locked on him from beneath his leg.

Scared the fuck outta Turner for real.

Wiping his mouth with the back of his hand, suddenly the wind picked up, the trees swayed heavy as he moved closer.

"You good?"

Silence.

After ruining the man's world, Turner said, "So...uh...where you live right now?"

Jalen frowned. "Why you asking me that, nigga?"

"Because if I was you I wouldn't tell Tink shit about your whereabouts."

"Is that right?" Jalen said, his voice low. "Good thing you ain't me."

"That was mean. I'm looking out for you."

"And why you wanna do that?"

Suddenly Jalen's gaze dropped, taking in the clothing Turner was wearing. A hoodie too big for his frame, its hem frayed and the fabric slightly stained.

"So what you gonna do? Because at the end of the day, me and you brothers. So—."

Turner opened his mouth to speak further when Jalen's hand moved. The gunshot was quick and when Turner caught the bullet, he staggered back, his eyes wide.

He tried to speak, but only a faint gurgle came out as blood oozed from his chest.

Jalen stepped closer, watching as Turner crumpled to the ground. The metallic scent of blood in the air as life drained from him. In a matter of seconds, Turner's body hit the cold earth hard.

For a moment, Jalen stood over him, his expression calm and detached. "Should've loved me more." He whispered.

After killing his own brother, he slipped the gun back into his jacket, glanced around to ensure the area was clear, and disappeared into the shadows, leaving Turner's lifeless body sprawled in a closed park like roadkill.

The room smelled slightly of vanilla, the soft mist of Breanna's shower still hanging in the air. Her new Persian cat, white as snow, purred at her ankles, its delicate fur brushing against her damp legs.

She stepped out of the bathroom wrapped in a plush white towel, her skin warm and dewy from the steam. When she opened the door, she saw Jalen standing in the middle of the room, his shoulders slumped, a long black raincoat draped over his thin frame. She forgot she gave his ass a key.

But what was he wearing?

It wasn't raining, but he wore it anyway, the edges brushing the floor.

His hands were buried deep in his pockets, and tears rolled down his face silently.

She paused.

Something about the way he stood there, unmoving, made her stomach twist. "What's wrong with you?" She asked, her voice soft as she approached him.

Jalen's eyes flicked up to meet hers, glassy and distant. "What is it about women and their ability to pull back...or hold back love?"

Breanna's tension eased slightly. She reached up, placing her warm hands gently on either side of his face. Her thumbs brushed over his cheeks, smearing away the tears as her gaze softened.

"You're wrong," she said quietly, leaning in to press a soft kiss to his lips. The faint, sour tang of vomit lingered on his breath, but she ignored it. When she pulled back, her grin returned, easy and practiced. "I'm not holding back love for you anymore."

Her hands slid down his jawline. "You replaced my cat. You're going to get me out of this neighborhood. Who couldn't love that?"

Jalen's expression darkened slightly as his hands stayed buried in his coat pockets. "So...if I didn't do all those things, you wouldn't love me?"

Breanna tilted her head, her thumb brushing the corner of his eye to catch a lingering tear. "For a girl like me, you have to pay what you owe," she whispered. "I mean look baby," she raised her arms, "I'm out of your league. You know that."

The phrase sliced through him like a blade, dragging him back to memories he couldn't outrun...his mother's voice, sharp and certain.

His breathing grew heavier, his fingers curling into fists inside the coat pockets.

Breanna didn't notice.

Instead, she smoothed a hand over his cheek, with amusement. But then she froze.

He stabbed her.

Her expression shifted in an instant, confusion bleeding into pain as her hands dropped to her stomach. She stumbled back, revealing the blood spreading across the white fabric.

The cat hissed, darting away as drops of crimson splattered its fur. Breanna backed up until her legs hit the edge of the bed, her knees giving out as she collapsed onto the mattress.

"Why?" She whispered, her voice trembling as her eyes locked on Jalen.

He stepped closer, his movements deliberate, almost tender. Once over her, he leaned down and pressed a soft kiss to her forehead as her breathing grew shallow, her eyes fluttering closed.

"Exactly," he said, his voice devoid of emotion. "Why?"

Breanna fell back, her body limp, the blood soaking into the sheets beneath her. Jalen straightened, his face blank, his hands sliding out of his coat pockets as he turned and walked out of the room.

Jalen stepped into Carl Stump's house, the smell hitting him like a wall. The air was thick with the odor of cat feces and rotting trash, so strong it made his eyes burn.

A white cat scattered and pissed as he moved through the narrow pathways of junk, their bodies darting across the dimly lit room. He didn't care about the filth. His focus was on the blind man sitting in the recliner, smiling faintly as if he knew Jalen was there before a word was spoken.

"What is it with you and cats?" Jalen said, shaking his head.

"I know why you here. And ain't no need in you doing it," Carl said, his voice calm, almost resigned.

"What you talking about?" Jalen replied, the long black raincoat making him look like a shadow in the chaos.

"I'm already dying," Carl said, lifting his shirt to reveal a gaping wound, red and oozing with infection.

Jalen's lip curled in disgust. "Why would you sit like this without getting help?"

"Because I don't trust nobody. Never have," Carl said with a dry chuckle. "Just like you, son."

"You nothing like me," Jalen snapped. "If I had a son—"

"You are incapable of loving," Carl interrupted, his voice firm but not unkind. "And that's okay, as long as you know and leave others be. But you can't can you? You gotta make others pay for the cards you believed you were dealt." He sighed. "You know, I showed up to your mother's house a few years back in the hopes of apologizing to you. To let you know I'm sorry for not being in your life. But I know you don't care. Do you?"

Jalen stared at him, his fists clenching at his sides. "You not even worth the bullet."

"You're right about that," Carl said softly, leaning back into the chair. "But you need to know...your mother cared about you in her own way."

"Fuck you and the bitch too. Tell her I'm sending everybody else she love in a minute." Jalen walked out, the stench of the house clinging to him as he left.

An hour later, Carl died.

CHAPTER SIXTEEN

In the apartment she shared with Davis, Memory's phone buzzed in her hand, and her heart jumped as Lockland's name flashed across the screen. She had just woken up from a nap but swallowed hard when she saw his name. For starters she had yet to do what Davis asked, by telling Lockland to meet her there.

Something felt off so she decided quietly against his request.

"Lockland?" She whispered, glancing nervously toward the bedroom door where Davis was rummaging through drawers.

His voice was low and strained. "Turner's dead. Jalen killed him."

Upon hearing those words, the world seemed to tilt beneath her, her breath catching in her throat. She gripped the phone tightly, her knees threatening to give way. "What? How?"

"No time to explain," Lockland interrupted. "But you need to get away from Davis. Now."

Memory's lips parted, but no sound exited. She glanced at the door again, dread creeping up her spine.

"But he was gonna ask you to marry me. He was gonna—."

"Memory," Lockland said firmly. "Meet me right now. Get out of that house. And do it fast."

She nodded even though he couldn't see her. "Okay," she whispered.

The call ended, and she stared at the dark screen for a moment, her mind racing. The bedroom door creaked open, and Davis emerged, his eyes narrowing as he saw her standing frozen in the middle of the room.

"Who was that?" He asked, his tone casual but carrying an edge.

"Lockland," she said quickly.

Davis crossed his arms, leaning against the doorway. "So, he gonna come over here, right? Like we talked about?"

Memory nodded, forcing herself to meet his gaze. "Yeah. Just...just like we planned."

Davis studied her for a moment longer, then shrugged. "Good. That's what I wanna hear." His eyes flicked toward the trash can by the door. "Oh...uh...since you up, take out the garbage."

"Oh...okay." With a tight grip on the bag, she moved to the door, her hands slick with sweat. "I'll be back."

"I know. Why wouldn't you be?" Davis shrugged, his attention already drifting elsewhere.

Memory stepped out of the apartment, the door clicking shut behind her. The cool night air hit her like a slap, as she descended the stairs slowly.

As she reached the bottom, she paused, glancing over her shoulder. The building was a bit behind her now and she wondered if Davis was watching.

Her breathing quickened as she tightened her grip on the trash bag. Instead of heading to the dumpster by the alley, she turned suddenly and began walking toward the street. Her pace quickened with each step until she was practically jogging, the trash bag swinging at her side.

By the time she reached the corner, she dropped the bag and broke into full runner's mode. The sound of her sneakers pounding against the pavement echoed.

She was gone.

The new cargo container sat in the middle of the deserted lot, its metal walls streaked with rust and grime. Inside, the air was heavy as Jalen sat alone on an overturned crate, his posture rigid, his fingers drumming softly against his knees.

Before taking out Turner and Breanna, he wasn't sure if he was capable of killing Lockland.

Now he knew he was, and he was suddenly unsure what else he was capable of in the future.

He reasoned at this point, that nothing was off the table.

The sound of footsteps crunching on gravel broke the silence. Jalen's head turned slightly as Tink stepped into the container. He hesitated in the doorway for a moment his usual swagger replaced with an uneasy tension.

"When did you move here?"

"I had to move. Lockland found the other spot."

Tink nodded. "Oh...oh he did?"

Jalen glared. "Yeah...he did."

"So you said you wanted to talk to me?"

"Why the rush?" Jalen didn't move, his gaze fixed on Tink like a predator sizing up its prey.

"No rush."

"Good...but let me ask you something...you seen Lockland?"

Tink blinked rapidly, the inquiry clearly catching him off guard. "Nah. Why would I see that nigga?" He replied, shrugging as if the question didn't matter.

Jalen's expression didn't change, but something in his eyes darkened.

He knew Tink was lying and more than anything it hurt. Turner had shown him the video, so he knew the man was a fraud. But he was still uneasy on what to do. He was one of his closest friends.

Jalen and Tink stood standing in front of one another.

"So you gonna lie to me?"

Tink shifted on his feet, the silence stretching uncomfortably between them. "Man, I done already told you no. Why you keep asking anyway?"

Jalen moved slowly toward him, the crate creaking beneath him with each step. He turned away, pretending to consider Tink's answer as he paced a few steps toward the far wall.

Tink, sensing the tension easing, let out a short laugh and turned his back to find a spot to sit. "Listen, you gotta get you another crib. And you gotta stop living in the open like you a dog or something," he took a seat. "He's just a—"

The sharp crack of a suppressed gunshot cut him off mid-sentence. Tink froze, his body swaying slightly before crumpling to the floor. Blood pooled beneath him, dark and spreading quickly over the cold metal.

Jalen stood over the lifeless body, his face devoid of expression.

This one hurt more than with Turner, although not as much as Breanna.

He stared at Tink's still form for a long moment, his chest rising and falling with controlled breaths. Despite his hardened exterior, something deep inside him felt fractured. Through countless fights, deals, and victories on the streets, he had always been there. And now, he was nothing more than a heap of flesh on the floor.

One brief second of remorse and then it was over.

Jalen bent down and pulled the gun from Tink's waistband. "Should've just told the truth."

Unbeknownst to Jalen, Everett had been approaching the cargo container from the distance since he was also summoned. But after seeing the fate of his man, he stopped abruptly. His heart pounded as he witnessed Jalen crouching low, peering cautiously in the distance.

Everett sat in his car, the engine idling quietly, fingers tapping his steering wheel. Should he make the call? After what seemed like no time, he decided the answer would be yes.

He yanked his cell, his hands trembling slightly, and dialed Jalen's number. "Where you at?" He paused. "I'm waiting."

"I'm still in route. Real quick though, I'm looking for Tink. You know where he is?"

Silence.

Jalen responded, his tone casual. "Nah, I haven't seen him in days. You either, to tell you the truth. That's what I wanted to rap to you about."

Everett nodded to himself. He could feel the lie in Jalen's voice. "Aight then...I'll get up with him later."

"Oh yeah, you definitely will," Jalen said.

Everett frowned, catching the meaning. Low key it had him fucked up in ways he didn't want to admit. But there was another story that troubled him. One that Lockland told him about his daughter after collecting him at the pool. And since it was vaguely close to the incident where he killed the whistler, but used Memory as bait, he needed to know the truth. Because Jalen always pretended that he would never do anything to harm his sister or any other child.

And to be clear, this was Everett's limit. He had three little girls who he adored and wasn't about the fuck shit when it came to kids.

"Listen, I never got around to asking you something."

"Shoot," Jalen replied, the distant sound of movement on his end suggesting he was walking.

"You ever regret the carnival incident?" Everett asked, his words slow and deliberate. "When you accidently killed Lockland's little girl?"

The question hung in the air. For a moment, there was silence, broken only by the faint rustle of leaves in the distance. Then Jalen laughed, the sound sarcastic and humorless.

"Why would I give a fuck about that nigga's daughter?" His voice dripped with indifference. "She not my kid and nobody ever gave a fuck about me."

His words hit him hard because he assured him that the bullet was always for Lockland and now he was learning it was all a lie.

"What difference does it make anyway?" He asked.

"No difference."

"Aight then...I'll see you in a minute right?"

"Yep...you sure will."

The room was silent except for the slight hum of the overhead fan, its blades spinning sluggishly. Lockland sat in the corner of his mother's room, his head bowed, his hands clasped tightly in front of him. Before him, her body lay on the bed, her skin looking greyer than it had days earlier.

The faint smell of chemical preservatives lingered in the air.

His phone buzzed on the table beside him, its vibration breaking the stillness. He knew who it was. The funeral director. The man had been calling incessantly, each time sounding more concerned, more insistent.

Lockland could hear his words in his mind: *You can't keep her. You're breaking the law. If you don't return her, I'll have to involve the authorities.*

But Lockland hadn't answered.

Instead he paid a man to beat his ass which bought him so more time.

Taking a deep breath, he hit Memory again, as they were supposed to be meeting. So where was she?

Lockland pulled up to Wakes' house, the soft rumble of his engine cutting through the quiet night. The street was dark, except the glow of the porch light across the front yard. He killed the engine and stepped out, the cool night air brushing against his skin. His boots crunched softly on the gravel as he approached the door. But before he could knock, it opened, and Wakes stood there, his expression unreadable.

"Come in."

Lockland nodded and entered. The living room was sparsely lit, and he saw Dion stretched out on the couch, a plate of half-eaten wings balanced on the coffee table in front of him. He glanced up as Lockland entered but said nothing.

For five minutes, silence hung in the air, heavy and unspoken. Lockland sat down in a worn armchair, his elbows resting on his knees, his hands clasped tightly together. His gaze skimmed between Wakes and Dion, his thoughts swirling. Finally, he leaned back, exhaling deeply.

"My bad," he said, breaking the silence. His voice was low but steady.

Wakes and Dion exchanged a glance but said nothing. They didn't need to. They both knew those two words were Lockland's way of apologizing...a rare thing.

And it was enough for them.

"I didn't move like I should have," Lockland continued after a moment. His eyes dropped to the floor as he rubbed the back of his neck. "I tapped out after Jalen took her and—"

"Say no more," Wakes interrupted, his voice firm but understanding.

"Yeah, man, we get it," Dion added, sitting up and leaning forward. "We just want you to know we're on your side through all of this. It's always been that way and won't change now."

Lockland looked at them, his jaw tightening as he nodded. Their loyalty wasn't something he doubted, but hearing it said aloud eased something inside.

"Good," he said finally. "Because I been working on a plan."

"Just you?" Wakes said.

"Nah...that's why I'm here. I laid the groundwork but I wanna run it past y'all to be sure it's solid. And it involves me trusting outsiders."

The salty air of the docks was thick and cool, carrying the scent of fish and rusted metal. Jalen stood near the edge, the waves lapping against the ships. He was thinking about what would happen next. Trying to remember back in the day when he and the young Lockland was close.

He had to finally admit, he didn't remember much about him.

And that gave Lockland an advantage.

When it got colder, he pulled his coat tighter against the breeze, his phone clutched loosely in his hand. The screen lit up with a name he hadn't expected.

Lockland.

Jalen smirked as he swiped to answer.

Lockland said, "Killed your own people huh?"

Jalen smiled and loved that he heard the news. "Don't know what you talking about."

"I hear you."

"Why you calling?"

"To tell you I'm sorry."

The smirk faded from Jalen's face. "For what? Not giving back the cat?"

"The moment I picked it up, I dropped it over your father's house. You ain't go over there when you know he got all them cats?"

Jalen felt dumb for not thinking straight. Of course Carl would have helped him out. "What you sorry about then?"

"I said I'm sorry," Lockland repeated. "I'm sorry for putting ma in a predicament where she chose me. I'm sorry for turning Memory and Turner against you. And I'ma get out of your lives. I just need to tell Memory face to face first. You know where she is?"

Jalen's grin returned, wider now. He remembered the occasion when he wanted to meet with Memory at the restaurant and Lockland chose to give him a hard time.

Should he return the favor? He leaned casually against a metal railing, his gaze sweeping over the dark waters below. "I do know where she is. But are you willing to do anything to get her?"

Silence hung in the air briefly.

"Anything."

Jalen chuckled softly. "Even a public message? You know, something nice. Letting the streets know you can't fuck with me."

There was a brief pause before Lockland replied, his tone clipped. "I said anything."

"Good," Jalen said, his grin widening. He straightened, his free hand drumming lightly against the railing. "Here's what you're gonna do. Send me that message and give me fifteen grand. You do that, and you can have her back."

"Don't hurt her," Lockland said quickly, his voice tightening with barely restrained panic. "Please."

"Hurt her?" Jalen repeated, his tone feigning offense. "Come on now. You know me better than that. I'd never hurt a little girl in my life."

The music thumped through Antonio's house, bass-heavy and rattling the windows. The air was thick with cheap cologne, liquor, and smoke from a few half-hidden blunts being passed around. People laughed, talked shit and sang along with the sounds coming from the Bluetooth speaker.

Antonio sat in the corner of his spacious living room, a drink in hand. Suddenly the front door swung open, and Jalen walked inside, his presence immediately drawing attention. Dressed in that black raincoat, a few people turned their heads and whispered. Besides, it had been well over a year since he showed his face out in public.

Jalen ignored them all, making a beeline for Antonio as if he were a mailman.

"What up, J?" Antonio said, raising his glass in greeting. "Didn't expect you to come out tonight. Figured you were still hiding."

Jalen smirked, pulling his phone from his pocket as he dropped into the chair across from Antonio. "Had to stop by and let y'all know the nigga caved."

Antonio took a sip of his drink. "What you mean?"

Jalen unlocked his phone and held it up, playing the video. In it was Lockland apologizing for fucking with him and saying the war was over on his end.

When the video ended, Antonio leaned back in his chair and chuckled, unamused. To be honest he could've showed him that in a text message.

"You see that?" Jalen said, his grin wide as he locked eyes with Antonio. "He don't want it with me."

Antonio's face remained neutral as he took another sip of his drink. "He fucking with you."

Jalen's grin faded.

Antonio shrugged, his voice calm but firm. "If he's doing all that, you should be more scared than ever."

The room quieted slightly, the weight of Antonio's words sinking into the air. Jalen shifted in his seat.

"I get it now. You scared of him not me." Jalen said, his tone edged with mockery. "But just so you know, even if he try something, I still got a plan in the works."

"Scared? Nah. But I respect his game. And from where I'm sitting, Lockland's playing it better than you are."

"Why you say that?"

"He took your mother, your brother, your sister and he got you outside. I mean how you know a hit not on your head?" He took a sip of his drink.

"Anybody can be after you...maybe even somebody in here."

Jalen and his black raincoat bounced shortly thereafter.

Jalen moved cautiously toward Davis' door. His boots echoed against the scuffed hardwood floors. When he reached it, he didn't hesitate. He raised a fist and banged three times.

The muffled sound of movement came from inside and a moment later, the door creaked open, and Davis' face appeared.

"Where's my sister?" Jalen asked, his voice low but carrying a dangerous edge. "She getting him here or what?"

"I keep forgetting y'all related."

"Where is she? Because I'm tired of waiting on this plan. You said you had it handled."

Davis hesitated, swallowing hard before offering a tight smile. "Come inside."

Jalen raised an eyebrow, but he stepped forward, his boots crossing the threshold. Davis locked the door behind him and walked a few feet away.

"Fuck you lock the door for? I ain't staying too long."

When Jalen turned back toward the room, his breath got caught up in his chest. He unknowingly walked into a trap. Because standing in his face was his long-lost nemesis, Lockland, propped up against the wall. Dion stood beside him, his massive frame blocking the only window as both men stared at Jalen, their expressions ice.

"Got you, ghost," Lockland said smiling.

Before Jalen could hit him, Dion lunged forward, his movements swift for a man of his size. His thick hands clamped down on Jalen's arms, pressing them behind his back. The force sent Jalen stumbling, his shoulder slamming into the wall.

Wakes sat in the driver's seat of the old sedan, scanning the park through the windshield. Beside him, Myra adjusted the scarf around her neck, her gaze fixed at a single person on a park bench.

"There she is," Myra said softly. "She looks scared."

Wakes nodded.

Memory sat hunched forward, her arms wrapped tightly around herself as if trying to shrink from the world. Her head moved left and right, like a cornered animal searching for a way out.

Slowly he pulled the car to the curb and for a moment, they sat in silence.

After several minutes, he stepped out of the car and opened the back door. The cool night air rushed in, but she didn't. Besides, she called her brother to scoop her up so why was he there?

From her place on the bench, Memory's eyes locked onto Wakes'. Glancing around, her gaze lingered on the empty streets and the darkened buildings.

No one else was going to save her.

She had to trust him.

She had to trust Lock.

Slowly, she stood, her legs shaky as she took a step forward. Her movements were hesitant, each motion heavier than the last. When she reached the open car door, she paused, her hand hovering over the edge.

Wakes didn't say a word.

He simply nodded toward the seat, his expression calm but leaving no room for argument.

When she was inside she saw Myra and asked, "Where am I going?"

"To Shannon's."

The van idled quietly in the parking lot outside Davis' building, its engine rumbling as Lockland and Dion secured Jalen inside. Two men, armed and watchful, stood near the entrance, their eyes scanning for any signs of trouble. Lockland slammed the back doors shut. And as he turned toward the driver's side, his eyes caught a familiar silhouette in the distance.

Grace.

"I'm sick of this bitch," he whispered his voice laced with frustration.

Dion glanced up from the passenger seat and glared. "Who you talking about?"

Lockland nodded toward the car parked under the hazy glow of a streetlamp. "Let me go see what's up."

Before he could move, Dion held out a hand. "Give me your hammer. I left mine at the crib."

"You always forgetting your gun," he said, shaking his head as he handed over the weapon. "This the last time."

Dion smirked, tucking the gun into his waistband. "You been saying that for years."

Lockland was already walking across the lot, his boots echoing against the asphalt. His annoyance grew with each step, the cool night air doing little to calm his nerves. When he reached Grace's car, he knocked on the window abruptly, hard enough to break the bitch.

She rolled it down.

"Fuck you doing here?" Lockland demanded, his voice low and tight.

"You been missing our meetings. When I told you what I needed from you."

"Yeah but I thought I told you not to follow me either."

"When you broke the contract, it meant all deals were off."

"You threatening me?"

This time, she didn't respond immediately. Instead, she tilted her head slightly and two men came up behind him.

He barely had time to process her statement before he felt the cold press of a gun barrel against his back. His muscles tensed, his instincts screaming at him to move, but the weight of two men flanking him froze him in place. He glanced over his shoulder, catching a glimpse of their hard, expressionless faces.

These weren't cops.

So who were they?

When he looked back toward the van, his heart sank. Eight men now surrounded Dion and them too, their weapons trained on the vehicle. What a difference a few seconds made. Because Jalen was no longer inside. Instead he stood in front of the group, his expression smug as he leaned casually against the side of the van.

And then he saw a body...it was two men carrying Davis' corpse to the trunk.

"So this what cops do?" Lockland asked, his voice dripping with hate.

Grace's smile widened, but there was no humor in it. "I'm not a cop," she said simply. "I never told you that. You just tend to finish people's sentences. Maybe you shouldn't do that in the future." She laughed. "Hold up, you don't have a future."

Lockland's jaw clenched, his mind racing as he tried to assess the situation. "If you were going to do this, why didn't you just kill me?"

"You always had your hand on your gun." Grace leaned slightly out of the window, her eyes glinting with something cold and unrecognizable. "But you not strapped now are you?"

She was right.

Dion had his gun.

Grace nodded to the men behind him. "Take him away."

Wakes drove quietly down the vaguely lit street. Memory sat in the backseat, her knees pulled to her chest, her arms wrapped tightly around herself. Myra was in the passenger seat, her sharp eyes scanning the road ahead.

The night air was thick, and the only sound was the occasional shuffle of Memory shifting in her seat and the low hum of the car engine. Wakes glanced at the rearview mirror, catching Memory's distant gaze as she stared out the window.

"It's gonna be aight," Wakes said, his voice calm but firm. "We'll get you where you need to be."

Memory didn't respond, but fear was evident. Sensing this, Myra reached back, her hand resting briefly on Memory's knee, offering silent reassurance.

But the calm shattered in an instant.

Out of nowhere, three black SUVs roared onto the street, their engines growling as they flanked the car. Headlights flooded the interior, bright and blinding, that danced across their faces.

"Damn it," Wakes said, gripping the wheel tighter. "We got company."

Myra turned quickly in her seat. "I think they after her. This nigga really wants all his family dead."

"Well, they gonna have to kill us first," Wakes replied, voice steady but full of anger.

The first SUV surged forward, pulling alongside them. A man leaned out of the passenger window, his face obscured by a ski mask and raised a weapon. The sudden flash of gunfire lit up the night, the loud cracks of bullets shattering the silence.

"Get down!" Wakes yelled as he swerved hard to the right, narrowly avoiding a barrage of bullets.

Myra didn't hesitate.

She pulled her pistol from the glove compartment, rolled down her window, and returned fire, the deafening shots ringing out into the night. The scent of gunpowder filled the car as Memory screamed to the top of her lungs. While also ducking lower in her seat as the chaos unfolded around her.

"You good, Myra?" Wakes shouted, his eyes flicking between the road and the rearview mirror.

"Just drive, nigga!" She yelled back, her voice tight as she fired off another round, the kick of the gun jolting her arm. One of the SUVs veered off slightly, its windshield shattered by her shot, but the others pressed on.

They were trying their best to get to her.

The chase intensified, the sound of screeching tires and blaring horns reverberating through the narrow streets. Wakes pushed the car to its limits, weaving through traffic and taking sharp turns that sent Memory sliding across the backseat like a ragdoll.

It was starting to look like they were out of harm's way, but he saw something else.

"Hold on!" Wakes shouted, gripping the wheel with white-knuckled determination.

Another SUV pulled up beside them, its front bumper grazing their car. Myra turned, her aim steady, and fired as many as she could before reloading. The SUV swerved wildly before crashing into a parked car, its hood crumpling like paper.

But the rest was short-lived.

A sharp turn ahead caught Wakes off guard, and the car skidded uncontrollably, tires squealing as they crashed into a streetlight. The impact jolted them violently, the airbags deploying with a muffled *slam*.

Smoke billowed from the hood, the scent of burning rubber filling the air. Wakes coughed, his chest heaving as he shoved the deflated airbag aside. "Everybody aight?"

"I'm good," Myra said, her voice shaky but strong. She turned to the backseat. "Memory?"

"I'm okay," she whispered. She clutched her arm, which was bruised but not broken.

"Aight," Wakes said, pulling himself out the car. He glanced around, his eyes scanning the shadows for any signs of the attackers. "We need to move. Now."

Blood trickled from a gash on Wakes' forehead, but he ignored it. While Myra grabbed her bag, tucking her gun into her waistband, and helped

Memory climb out of the wreckage. Together, they slipped into the darkness of a nearby side street, the sound of distant sirens growing louder.

The cargo box on the Baltimore docks was eerily quiet. Inside, Lockland and Dion sat tied to heavy metal chairs, the ropes cutting into their wrists. Both men were battered but unbroken, their eyes scanning the room, taking in every detail.

Jalen stood before them, his arms crossed, satisfaction all across his face.

"Look at this," Jalen began, his voice arrogant. "The great Lockland Logan, tied up like a dog. Never thought I'd see the day."

Lockland stayed silent, his expression calm, his eyes steady. Dion, however, growled through gritted teeth, struggling against his restraints. "When I get out of this—"

"You won't do shit," Jalen interrupted. "You won't. None of you will this time."

"You so cocky," Lockland said. "Maybe you shouldn't be though."

"Nah, fake bro," Jalen began pacing, his footsteps echoing through the cargo box. "You thought you could come after me, but it didn't work. I don't know why I hid as long as I did." He shook his head. "If only the world could see you now. Tied up, helpless, and waiting to die."

Lockland's faint smile made Jalen pause. "You talk a lot for a man who wouldn't last two minutes in a real fight."

Jalen stopped, narrowing his eyes. "What did you just say?"

"I said you wouldn't last two minutes boxing against me," Lockland repeated, his voice calm but taunting. "You can't even beat me now without your boys backing you up."

"I'm not playing these games."

"You scared, Jalen?"

The room grew quieter, the tension shifting. A few of Jalen's men exchanged glances.

"Nigga, I never been scared of you before and I'm not scared of you now."

"You didn't say that when I whipped your ass when we were kids."

"Not kids though...We men now."

"Word? Then prove it," Lockland said, leaning forward as much as his restraints would allow. "Untie me. Let's go one-on-one."

A ripple of unease passed through Jalen's men, their loyalty wavering as curiosity took hold. One of them whispered loud enough for Jalen to hear, "He's got a point, boss. You can take him. Trust me. He look high as fuck anyway. Burnt the fuck out."

Jalen's ego flared.

He motioned for one of his men to untie Lockland. "Fine. Remember this your fault. If you ask me it's stupid to start a fight just to die."

Dion growled, his eyes narrowing as he watched Lockland rise from the chair, rolling his shoulders to loosen the stiffness. "You sure about this, Lock?"

Lockland gave him a slight nod, his eyes never leaving Jalen. "I'm 'bout to kill this nigga."

The fight began. Jalen swung first, his punches wild and fueled by jealousy. Lockland dodged easily, his footwork precise. Each missed punch left Jalen more unbalanced, more exposed, mainly because he threw his entire body at him just to be annoyed.

Then Lockland struck.

A quick, brutal jab to Jalen's ribs that sent him stumbling back. The men watching erupted into shouts and whispers, their loyalty shaken further with each precise blow Lockland landed.

Now he wished he left the nigga locked up because this was quite embarrassing.

Jalen growled, tried to bite his face and even stepped on his toe. Coupled with wild punches he appeared out of his league. Throwing one last hail Mary, he caught him as he leaned forward. This time, Lockland caught it bad, twisting Jalen's arm and sending him crashing to the ground with a heavy thud.

"Stay down," Lockland said, his voice steady.

Jalen's men surged forward to help, but suddenly, the sound of a gunshot stopped them in their tracks. Everett stepped into the cargo box, his gun raised, his presence commanding. When he saw the men moving like they were gonna snatch him, he said, "I wouldn't do that if I were you."

The room froze.

Everett's eyes swept over the scene.

"Took you long enough," Lockland replied, wiping blood from the corner of his mouth. "I had to fight this nigga just to stall." Next he grabbed a gun tucked on Everett's other side. Now armed, he turned to Jalen's men, his voice cold. "Drop your weapons. Now."

They hesitated, but the sight of Everett's unwavering aim and the fire in Lockland's eyes convinced them that fighting for Jalen wasn't worth it. He was a bum anyway.

One by one, the weapons clattered to the floor. Dion was also freed.

With Jalen subdued and his men wrapped up, Everett lowered his gun and stepped back. "I did my part," he said to Lockland, his voice steady. "I'm out."

Lockland nodded. "Fair enough. The money is at the spot."

"I already got it," he winked.

As Everett disappeared into the shadows, Lockland pulled out his phone and made a call. "It's done," he said simply before hanging up.

Minutes later, the sound of an approaching car, followed by heels, echoed through the dockyard. Shannon stepped into the cargo box, her eyes locking onto Jalen. Her expression was calm, but there was a storm in her gaze ready to be unleashed.

"Shannon," Jalen said, his voice faltering for the first time.

She didn't reply. Instead, she removed a gun from her purse, raised it and aimed steady. "This is for Asia."

A shot tore through his left arm, followed by another that hit his right. Jalen screamed, the sound raw and filled with pain. The next shot struck his left leg, and then the right, dropping him to the ground. With a woman's work done, she tucked her gun back into her purse.

With Jalen moaning on the ground she walked toward him. "I want you to know, that your jealous ass didn't break me." She looked at the blood pouring from his body. "But I broke you."

"Fuck you," he cried, spit flying from his mouth. "Fuck you!"

"You know what, I used to feel sorry for you. Maybe Cakes didn't do right by you. Maybe she didn't love you right. But Lockland did, and you hated him for it."

She stood up and kissed Lockland. "Finish it, baby."

"You ain't got to do this man," Jalen said. "You ain't got to do it."

"I have to...you a ghost, remember?" Lockland shot him in the center of his head and watched the life drain from his body.

Wakes and Lockland approached Larry's door.

The air smelled faintly of rain, though the storm had passed hours ago, leaving a damp chill clinging to everything. Lockland raised his hand and knocked once, loud and deliberate.

Seconds later, Larry opened the door almost immediately, his face heavy with the loss of his only son.

If they were there, he didn't need them to say a word. One look at their faces told him everything he needed to know. Without hesitation, he grabbed his jacket from the chair by the door and followed them to the truck.

When Lockland opened the back of the Yukon, Larry froze for a moment. There, just as promised, was Jalen's lifeless body, laid out like a final offering.

He turned to Lockland and Wakes, his hand resting firmly on each of their shoulders. When the trunk was closed, he turned and walked back into his house.

Grace stepped out of the bathroom; her body wrapped in a soft pink cotton robe. Steam billowed, clinging to the cool air of the apartment. She walked barefoot across the hardwood floors, her hair damp and hugging her neck.

Her movements were hurried as she entered her bedroom, pulling a suitcase from the closet and setting it on the bed. With trembling hands, she began grabbing clothes and stuffing them inside without care for organization.

And so she was slipping.

She didn't hear him at first.

The creak of her own rocking chair in the corner of the room was swallowed by her heavy breathing. It wasn't until she turned, suitcase in hand, that her eyes landed on the figure seated calmly in the shadows.

Dion.

Her breathing stopped, and the suitcase slipped from her grasp, landing on the floor with a loud thump. She clutched her chest, her heart pounding so loudly it drowned out everything else.

"I see you packing," Dion said, his voice low and steady. He stood, the lamp shining on the gun in his hand. "But where you going, you won't need luggage."

Tears welled in Grace's eyes as she took a shaky step back, her legs brushing against the bed. "You don't...don't understand," she stuttered, her voice breaking. "He made me do it."

Dion's expression didn't change.

His eyes were cold.

"Not trying to hear it," he said, cutting her off, while stepping closer "Because we would've taken care of you."

Her knees buckled, and she sank onto the edge of the bed, her hands trembling. "Please," she whispered, her voice barely audible. "I didn't have a choice. Don't kill me just because Jalen made me do it."

Dion stared down at her, not giving a fuck about her begging. "Before I finish all this, I need you to tell me one thing. If you don't tell me your death will be torturous. If you do, it'll be as painless as possible."

"You want some pussy at least? To keep me alive."

"Nah, I'm good on that."

Defeated, and with limited options, Grace nodded slowly. "Okay...okay, what do you want to know."

"When Jalen was staying in that ambulance, were did he keep his shit? I'm looking for something."

Lockland stood in front of the rusted metal door of unit #47 of an outside storage unit, his breath visible in the cold night air. His hand rested on the heavy padlock, but he made no move to open it.

Footsteps echoed softly behind him, steady and familiar. Lockland didn't turn; he didn't need to. Moments later, Dion came to a stop beside him, and he didn't speak.

Lockland understood immediately what was unsaid.

Grace was gone.

Good riddens.

Taking a deep breath, Lockland pulled a key from his pocket and inserted it into the lock. After a few attempts it clicked open. The screech of the roller drowned out the silence as the storage unit revealed itself.

The first thing that hit him was the smell.

Stale, musty, the unmistakable scent of things long forgotten. The front part of the unit was cluttered with some luxurious furniture, appliances, and boxes stacked any kind of way. Dust hung heavy in the air, catching the faint light from the single bulb overhead.

Lockland stepped inside, his boots crunching against scattered debris. He moved methodically, his sharp eyes scanning the chaos, pushing aside broken chairs and boxes. It didn't take long. Behind the mess, toward the back, was the sewing stand.

The sight stopped him in his tracks.

It was unmistakable, even through the layer of grime and time. The delicate carvings along the edges, the faint sheen of the polished wood. It was just as he remembered.

Dion stepped up behind him, and placed a hand on Lockland's shoulder, the gesture firm but silent, offering support without words.

"Let's get it out of here," Lockland said quietly.

EPILOGUE

The sun hung high in the sky, its warm rays spilling over the cemetery like a bittersweet blessing for Cakes' funeral. The gentle rustle of leaves in the breeze calmed everyone present. Lockland stood at the head of the casket, his broad frame stiff with emotion, as he stared down at the polished wood. His mother lay inside, her body finally at rest, her long journey coming to an end.

It was a beautiful day for something so dark.

Unlike Turner's funeral where it rained and stormed all day.

But not for Cakes.

For her the heavens put across a brilliant blue sky, scattered with soft clouds that seemed almost out of place.

Lockland glanced around, taking in the small crowd of family and friends who had come to honor his mother. Dion and Wakes stood to his left, their suits slightly wrinkled, but their loyalty unshaken. His aunt Myra stood beside them, her hands folded neatly in front of her, her face presenting a quiet strength. His sister, Memory, was to his right, her tear-streaked face buried in her hands as her shoulders shook with grief.

But it was the woman on his arm who made it all a little more bearable.

Shannon.

After everything they'd been through, they managed to find their way back to each other. Her presence lightened the burden he carried as his hand resting in hers became a silent reminder that he wasn't alone.

The minister spoke, his voice calm and steady, delivering words of comfort that drifted into the air. Lockland barely registered them, his mind heavy with the weight of the promises he had made and kept. The sewing stand, Memory's safety, settling the beefs in the streets...all of which he had done.

As the casket was lowered into the ground, Lockland felt a weird peace wash over him. His mother's words echoed in his mind, a mantra he had lived by through the storm: "Sooner or later, everybody pays what they owe." He had paid his dues, fulfilled his promises. For the first time in a long time, he allowed himself to hope that things might finally settle.

As if Shannon could read his mind, she leaned in, her voice soft but steady. "You did it, Lockland. You kept your word."

He turned to her and smiled. "I just hope she's at peace."

"She is," Shannon replied. "And she's here with you too."

The burial concluded, and one by one, the mourners began to leave, offering Lockland quiet condolences and firm handshakes. Dion clapped him on the shoulder as they walked away.

The house stood proudly on the quiet street; its once-faded exterior now restored to its former glory. The fresh coat of paint gleamed in the sunlight, the garden out front brimming with bright flowers and neatly trimmed hedges. It wasn't just a house anymore.

It was now a home.

Lockland's mother's house, rebuilt piece by piece, was a testament to the promises he kept and the life he was working to create.

Inside, the warm aroma of something baking in the oven caused everything to feel like home. Shannon stood in the kitchen, her hands resting on the gentle curve of her stomach, her glow unmistakable. She was pregnant again, and this time, it was a boy. She hummed softly to herself as she moved about, her voice blending with the distant sound of Memory's laughter echoing from the living room as she spoke on the phone.

Lockland sat at the sewing table in what used to be his mother's room, now transformed into a workspace. The sewing stand sat before him, polished and carefully restored, every detail meticulously maintained. His hands moved skillfully, threading the needle and stitching the fabric. He was working on a suit, his first official piece since taking up her craft.

This suit was special. It wasn't for a client or a friend, although he had recently opened a tailor's shop in Baltimore city.

Nah, this one was for himself.

In keeping with his mother's promise, the first suit he made would be his own. The dark navy fabric shimmered under the soft light of the room, each stitch a small act of homage to the woman who taught him everything he knew.

Shannon peeked inside, leaning against the doorframe with a soft smile. "How's it coming along?"

"Almost done," Lockland replied before winking. "It has to be perfect."

"It will be," she said, stepping closer and resting a hand on his shoulder.

He set the fabric down, turning his chair slightly to face her. "You sure you're okay with keeping it small? Just family and friends."

"That's all we need," she replied, her hand moving to rest on her belly. "It's not about the size. It's about getting married and starting our lives together."

The day of the ceremony came quickly, and the house buzzed with quiet excitement. The backyard had been transformed into a simple but elegant space, with white chairs arranged in neat rows and strings of lights hanging overhead. Memory hopped about, her bright laughter filling the air as she helped Aunt Myra arrange the final touches.

Lockland stood in front of the mirror, adjusting his tie. The suit fit perfectly, the navy fabric sharp against his broad frame. Every stitch, every seam, carried a piece of his mother's legacy. He took a deep breath.

Dion appeared in the doorway, a broad grin on his face. "Look at you, man. Smooth as hell."

Lockland turned, smirking. "You think?"

"Nigga, I said what I said. Ain't bout to tell you again," he laughed.

The ceremony itself was intimate but perfect. Friends and family gathered under the warm glow of the lights. Shannon walked down the aisle, radiant in her simple white dress, her hand resting lightly on her growing belly. Lockland's heart pumped as he watched her approach.

He didn't know what the future held, but for now, surrounded by love and family, he allowed himself to hope.

The sun poured through the wide front windows of *Lock and Threads*, casting warm light across the polished hardwood floors. The air was filled with the hum of chatter and the faint scent of fabric and starch, blending with the soft whir of the sewing machine in the back.

Lockland leaned casually against the counter, his sharp brown suit fitting him like a second skin. No shirt, per his own code, the diamond chain around his neck catching the light every time he moved.

Business was good.

His clientele was a mix of dope dealers, hustlers, and anyone with pockets deep enough to pay for his precision. He even had to push a nigga away who preferred what he could do with the gun instead of the needle.

When the doorbell jingled as another customer stepped in the shop, and Lockland's eyes moved up from the cufflinks he'd been polishing. The man who entered stopped just inside, his posture straight and confident, his tailored jacket hinting at someone used to being in control.

What struck Lockland most, though, was the familiarity of his face.

It wasn't just that he looked smooth…he looked eerily like *him*.

"I heard you were the best," the man said. "So here I am."

"That's what they say," Lockland nodded slowly, his jaw tightening as he studied the man. "What's the occasion?"

The man smiled. "I'm marrying your mother."

"My mother dead."

"Nah...she ain't."

He stepped to the side and Lockland froze, his blood running cold. In his waiting room, he spotted his mother sitting with his sister.

"Hey, baby boy," Tracey said, waving long painted read nails. "Remember me?"

Fuck.

UP NEXT

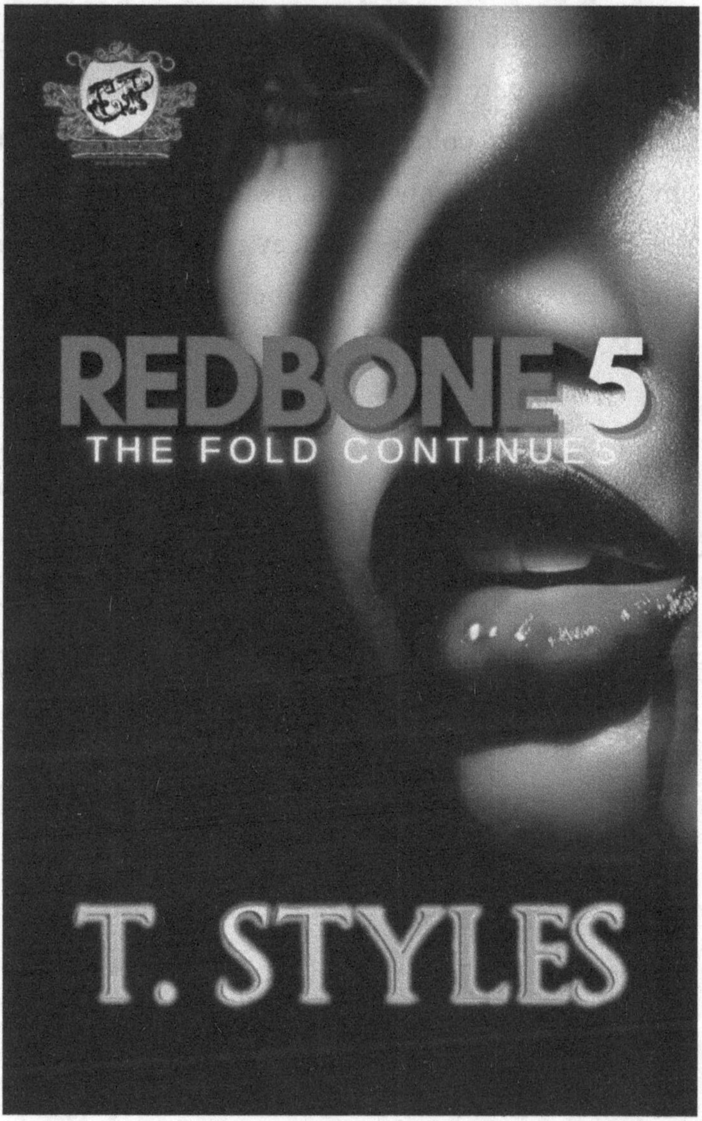

CARTEL PUBLICATIONS

PRESENTS

The Cartel Publications Order Form

www.thecartelpublications.com

Inmates **ONLY** receive novels for $14.00 per book **PLUS** shipping fee **PER BOOK.**

(Mail Order **MUST** come from inmate directly to receive discount)

Shyt List 1	________	$15.00
Shyt List 2	________	$15.00
Shyt List 3	________	$15.00
Shyt List 4	________	$15.00
Shyt List 5	________	$15.00
Shyt List 6	________	$15.00
Pitbulls In A Skirt	________	$15.00
Pitbulls In A Skirt 2	________	$15.00
Pitbulls In A Skirt 3	________	$15.00
Pitbulls In A Skirt 4	________	$15.00
Pitbulls In A Skirt 5	________	$15.00
Victoria's Secret	________	$15.00
Poison 1	________	$15.00
Poison 2	________	$15.00
Hell Razor Honeys	________	$15.00
Hell Razor Honeys 2	________	$15.00
A Hustler's Son	________	$15.00
A Hustler's Son 2	________	$15.00
Black and Ugly	________	$15.00
Black and Ugly As Ever	________	$15.00
Ms Wayne & The Queens of DC **(LGBTQ+)**	________	$15.00
Black And The Ugliest	________	$15.00
Year Of The Crackmom	________	$15.00
Deadheads	________	$15.00
The Face That Launched A Thousand Bullets	________	$15.00
The Unusual Suspects	________	$15.00
Paid In Blood	________	$15.00
Raunchy	________	$15.00
Raunchy 2	________	$15.00
Raunchy 3	________	$15.00
Mad Maxxx (4th Book Raunchy Series)	________	$15.00
Quita's Dayscare Center	________	$15.00
Quita's Dayscare Center 2	________	$15.00
Pretty Kings	________	$15.00
Pretty Kings 2	________	$15.00
Pretty Kings 3	________	$15.00
Pretty Kings 4	________	$15.00

Silence Of The Nine	______	$15.00
Silence Of The Nine 2	______	$15.00
Silence Of The Nine 3	______	$15.00
Prison Throne	______	$15.00
Drunk & Hot Girls	______	$15.00
Hersband Material **(LGBTQ+)**	______	$15.00
The End: How To Write A Bestselling Novel In 30 Days (Non-Fiction Guide)	______	$15.00
Upscale Kittens	______	$15.00
Wake & Bake Boys	______	$15.00
Young & Dumb	______	$15.00
Young & Dumb 2: Vyce's Getback	______	$15.00
Tranny 911 **(LGBTQ+)**	______	$15.00
Tranny 911: Dixie's Rise **(LGBTQ+)**	______	$15.00
First Comes Love, Then Comes Murder	______	$15.00
Luxury Tax	______	$15.00
The Lying King	______	$15.00
Crazy Kind Of Love	______	$15.00
Goon	______	$15.00
And They Call Me God	______	$15.00
The Ungrateful Bastards	______	$15.00
Lipstick Dom **(LGBTQ+)**	______	$15.00
A School of Dolls **(LGBTQ+))**	______	$15.00
Hoetic Justice	______	$15.00
KALI: Raunchy Relived (5th Book in Raunchy Series)	______	$15.00
Skeezers	______	$15.00
Skeezers 2	______	$15.00
You Kissed Me, Now I Own You	______	$15.00
Nefarious	______	$15.00
Redbone 3: The Rise of The Fold	______	$15.00
The Fold (4th Redbone Book)	______	$15.00
Clown Niggas	______	$15.00
The One You Shouldn't Trust	______	$15.00
The WHORE The Wind Blew My Way	______	$15.00
She Brings The Worst Kind	______	$15.00
The House That Crack Built	______	$15.00
The House That Crack Built 2	______	$15.00
The House That Crack Built 3	______	$15.00
The House That Crack Built 4	______	$15.00
Level Up **(LGBTQ+)**	______	$15.00
Villains: It's Savage Season	______	$15.00
Gay For My Bae **(LGBTQ+)**	______	$15.00
War	______	$15.00
War 2: All Hell Breaks Loose	______	$15.00
War 3: The Land Of The Lou's	______	$15.00
War 4: Skull Island	______	$15.00
War 5: Karma	______	$15.00
War 6: Envy	______	$15.00
War 7: Pink Cotton	______	$15.00
Madjesty vs. Jayden (Novella)	______	$8.99
You Left Me No Choice	______	$15.00
Truce – A War Saga (War 8)	______	$15.00
Ask The Streets For Mercy	______	$15.00
Truce 2 (War 9)	______	$15.00
An Ace and Walid Very, Very Bad Christmas (War 10)	______	$15.00
Truce 3 – The Sins of The Fathers (War 11)	______	$15.00
Truce 4: The Finale (War 12)	______	$15.00
Treason	______	$20.00
Treason 2	______	$20.00

Hersband Material 2 **(LGBTQ+)**	________	$15.00
The Gods Of Everything Else (War 13)	________	$15.00
The Gods Of Everything Else 2 (War 14)	________	$15.00
Treason 3	________	$15.99
An Ugly Girl's Diary	________	$15.99
The Gods Of Everything Else 3 (War 15)	________	$15.99
An Ugly Girl's Diary 2	________	$19.99
King Dom **(LGBTQ+)**	________	$19.99
The Gods Of Everything Else 4 (War 16)	________	$19.99
Raunchy: The Monsters Who Raised Harmony	________	$19.99
An Ugly Girl's Diary 3	________	$19.99
From Men To Monsters (War 17)	________	$19.99
Pretty Kings 5	________	$19.99
From Men To Monsters 2 (War 18)	________	$19.99
A Weird Peace	________	$19.99

(**Redbone 1** & **2** are **NOT** Cartel Publications novels and if **ordered** the cost is **FULL** price of $16.00 **each plus shipping**. **No Exceptions**.)

Please add **$8.00** for shipping and handling fees for up to **(2) BOOKS PER ORDER**. (INMATES INCLUDED) (See next page for details)

The Cartel Publications * P.O. BOX 486 OWINGS MILLS MD 21117

Name: ____________________

Address: ____________________

City/State: ____________________

Contact/Email: ____________________

Please allow 10-15 BUSINESS days Before shipping.

****PLEASE NOTE DUE TO **COVID-19** SOME ORDERS MAY TAKE UP TO **3 WEEKS OR LONGER** **BEFORE** THEY SHIP****

The Cartel Publications is NOT responsible for Prison Orders rejected!

NO RETURNS and NO REFUNDS
NO PERSONAL CHECKS ACCEPTED
STAMPS NO LONGER ACCEPTED

www.ingramcontent.com/pod-product-compliance
Lightning Source LLC
Chambersburg PA
CBHW011350010726
47494CB00008B/2253
* 9 7 8 1 9 4 8 3 7 3 9 8 2 *